SIMPLY
FOUR STORIES

Norma Iris Pagan Morales

ISBN 978-1-959895-82-4 (paperback)
ISBN 978-1-959895-81-7 (ebook)

Printed in the United States of America

DEDICATION

This book is dedicated to my sister, Adelin Milagros Pagan Morales. She is gone but not forgotten.

LOVE HAS NO AGE BOUNDARY

OVERVIEW

Mark nearly laughed aloud when Betty signaled at him for several tense seconds as if she was trying to search out the deeper meaning of his words. He could tell the moment she'd brushed his comment aside, as if it was a joke, by the slight shake of her head.

He wanted to grab hold of her and shake her. She was a brilliant woman, but for some reason she always chose to play dumb when it came to his obvious flirting and comments.

CHAPTER 1

Betty the Ice-Cold Bitch

Senior Vice President, Betty Smith, tread heavily angrily past the cubicles of her nosy employees, ignoring their probing stares and low snickers.

They could barely contain their joy. The Cold Bitch, as she was called, was finally gone. They thought she didn't know what they whispered behind her back, but she did. She knew everything the close to one hundred employees she supervised said about her.

They thought she was a sad, lonely, pathetic frigid bitch. Maybe they were right.

She'd worked for an International Hotel Corporation ever since she'd graduated from college.

Over the past twenty years, she'd steadily climbed the corporate ladder, sacrificing everything to achieve her goal and that is to become CEO of the largest hotel chain in the world.

She had always remained professional and distant from her employees, running her division with cool efficiency and precision. The marketing division was undoubtedly the most productive arm of the company. So, when AL Stone retired earlier that year as CEO, she'd been sure the job was hers.

She yanked open the door to her corner office with the amazing view of downtown area Brooklyn, stepped inside and slammed it behind her.

She wasted no time grabbing a Xerox box full of new stacks of paper.

Dumping the unopened packets to the floor, she began to clean out her desk.

As she carelessly stuffed her most personal belongings into the box, she replayed the words that had changed her life forever.

"…So, it is with great pride and enthusiasm that I introduce to you Stone's newest CEO, my grandson, Mark Stone." She had sat there stunned when the owner, Gerry Stone, had delivered the news to the twelve-member Board of Directors, the new CEO, Mark Stone, and to her.

She clenched her teeth at the thought of him. She was being grabbed by a twenty-nine-year-old Harvard Business graduate who'd only been with the company for two years.

He was barely out of grad school and now he was the CEO of a Fortune 500 Companies.

The sound of her office door closing caught her attention, and she turned around to face the last person she wanted to see.

"Betty, I'm sorry. I didn't know."

She held up her hand to halt his next words. "It's fine Mark Stone. I could tell from your shocked expression that it was news to you too. Still, congratulations," she said stiffly, before twisting back around to finish packing.

"I couldn't believe you stormed out of there. Hey, what are you doing?"

"What does it look like I'm doing?" she snapped as she continued to dump her things into the box.

She froze at the touch of his hand against her arm. Blowing out a long, jagged breath she turned around to face him. as soon as she let his gaze, and glimpsed the hurt look on his handsome face, she instantly regretted her terse words. It wasn't his fault.

Mark didn't deserve any of her anger. Ever since he'd joined the company two years ago, as the CFO, he'd been nothing but kind toward her, even though she'd always kept him at arm's length.

"Don't quit," he said softly.

She shrugged his hand from her arm, flashing him a weak smile. "I must."

"But I need you," he said, and she almost swore she saw something flash in his eyes that hinted at a more intimate need, but then it disappeared, and she figured it had just been her imagination. He cleared his throat. "To advise me. You have the most experience of any of the senior staff and I need your expertise."

"I'm sorry, Mark, but you know I can't stay," she said quietly, holding his penetrating blue gaze.

"What will you do?"

She shrugged as she curled her lips into a wry smile. "I don't know and for the first time in my life, I don't care." It was true. She had lived her life for so long always striving to accomplish her next goal.

Well, for the first time ever she had no goal and it felt good. The disappointment on his face tugged at her, and for just a moment she experienced a pain of guilt.

Feeling compelled to do something she was sure she would later regret, she grabbed one of her business cards and scribbled on the back. "Here is my home number. If you find you have a question, just call me."

She shoved her card into his hand and whirled back around to finish with her task. She heard him mumble "thanks" followed by the soft click of the door closing shut.

Contrary to what her employees thought, she did have feelings and she felt bad for dumping her anger on Mark when he'd had nothing to do with the events that had happened earlier.

But she couldn't help feeling an ache of resentment. He now held the position that she'd coveted for the last five years. Still, that had been no excuse for her abrupt dismissal and downright rude behavior. She toyed with the thought of going after him to apologize, but quickly abandoned the idea. He'd be fine.

She on the other hand wouldn't. The knowledge that she'd given up so much for a dream that had been snatched so cruelly from her was enough to send her increasing headfirst to depression.

Painful memories from the past twenty years of all the sacrifices she'd made replayed themselves in her head. The main one being from three years ago when her ex-fiancé walked out on her shortly after she'd miscarried their baby, all the while throwing accusations at her that her workaholic schedule had been the cause.

Now she knew that Tony was nothing but an asshole and a jerk, but at the time the pain and guilt had only driven her to work harder, making her even more determined to achieve the goal that had cost her the family she'd always wanted.

Tears burned the backs of her eyes, and she drew in a deep breath, as she forced them not to fall. She needed to hurry up and finish packing so that she could get out of there before she did what she so desperately longed to do it, slump to the floor, and indulge in a good cry.

But her pride would not allow her to give into the impulse. The Ice Bitch did not crack, and she certainly didn't melt.

Mark Stone flopped down in the plush leather cushions of his office chair and blew out a long breath.

How could his grandfather do this to Betty and to him even? He ran an angry hand through his close-cropped, jet-black hair, disheveling it into wild spikes. When Al retired, his grandfather assured him that Betty would be promoted to CEO. So, it had been a shock to him when his name had been announced instead.

Right after Betty stormed out, he pulled Mr. Stone aside for an explanation. "What was that about? You told me Ms. Smith was going to be promoted," he'd accused.

His grandfather had shrugged his stocky shoulders and the lines of his face had deepened when he'd spoken. He at least had the decency to appear remorseful.

"I wanted to promote her, but the Board refused to support her bid for CEO. They were uncomfortable with having someone from outside the family in the position again. I had no choice but to appoint you. I'm sorry Mark."

"It's not me you should be apologizing to," he'd whispered angrily before spinning on his heels to follow Betty.

He leaned back in his chair and stared out across Midtown; his eyes vacant. Betty didn't deserve this. She had devoted herself to Stone Corp, and this was her thanks. If he'd been her, he would have quit too.

He glanced down at the card in his hand, twisting it between his fingers. She'd given it to him and told him to call her if he had any questions. A small grin flashed across his face. He had a question. Would she have dinner with him Friday night?

That had been the main question he'd wanted to ask her since he'd first laid eyes on the luscious older woman two years ago.

He remembered their first meeting like it was yesterday. She'd been wearing a form fitting white turtleneck Cashmere dress that hugged her gorgeous figure down to her knees, where it teased the tops of her spike heeled black leather boots.

The soft white shade of the dress had complimented the warm tones of her rich, chocolate complexion. Her shoulder length hair had been pulled back into a plain bun and she'd worn standard wire rimmed glasses that obscured her beautiful almond shaped brown eyes.

She'd shaken his hand with cool authority, and he'd been smitten ever since. No matter how hard he tried to invite her to lunch or engage her in small talk, she had always remained polite, but remote.

The essence of professionalism. Everyone called her the Cold Bitch if they were nice, worse if they weren't. But he sensed beneath her chilly exterior was a warm and sensual woman who she worked very hard to hide, and it was that woman he wanted to discover.

He wanted to get to know the real Betty Smith, not the one she showed to the rest of the world.

He stared at the ten digits she'd hastily scrawled on the back of the card. What would she do if he called her and asked her out? Or better yet, showed up on her doorstep with an invitation to dinner?

He knew the answer to both of those questions. She would give him a cool, but polite, no.

If he wanted to get to know Betty more intimately, then he was going to have to come up with something far better than a phone call or a visit.

A thought popped into his head, and he sat up, sat straight, on his chair. It was a long shot, a crazy idea even. He curled his lips up into a smile and glanced back down at the card.

Crazy idea or not, he was fresh out of options. He shot up from his chair and bounded out of his office just in time to see the doors to the elevator close with Betty inside.

His smile grew wider. Perfect timing.

Chapter 2

The Lie

"That's impossible." Betty cried as her fingers skimmed across the keyboard of her office computer, her eyes frantic.

After several long minutes, she finally stopped and stirred her chair around, nearly throwing Mark off balance, who'd been leaning against it to look over her shoulder.

"I don't know what happened. When I left Thursday, it was here. I promise you."

"It was your account, Betty. If you don't have it, then no one else docs," Mark said coolly.

For several moments she just stared at him with flashing eyes, not really knowing what to say or do. She was at a complete loss.

When she'd cleaned out her desk two days ago, she had been sure to leave all company files on her computer or on disks in her office. It was company policy.

Once an employee ended his or her relationship with Stone, they were obligated by law, to leave all materials pertaining to Stone accounts at the office. It was to ensure that private information did not somehow end up in the hands of their competitors.

Betty hadn't broken the rules. She had left everything but her personal belongings at the office.

So, when she'd received a call from Mark saying that he couldn't locate the files for the New Zealand account anywhere on her computer or in her office, she'd raced down there on a Saturday still dressed in her

"Lounging at home on a Saturday morning" attire of faded jeans, flip flop sandals and a canary yellow tank top.

"I—I don't know what to tell you," She stammered. This had never happened to her before. She had never in her entire time at the company lost an account.

Mark straightened to his full height and of its own will, her gaze traced the outline of his rippling muscles that strained against his short sleeved white cotton t-shirt.

She swallowed the lump in her throat. He looked every bit as young as he was in what appeared to be his gym clothes. But he was still strikingly handsome.

She used every ounce of self-restraint not to let her eyes dip lower where she'd glimpsed the faint outline of his impressive cock through the thin material of his grey sweatpants when she first arrived. She was so used to seeing him in suits that his casual attire had jolted her.

Being there with him on a Saturday, in plain clothes, gave the meeting a slightly more intimate feel to it. She gulped down a deep breath, trying to ease the furious beating of her heart.

His closeness was unsettling in the closed space with just the two of them alone.

"We meet with the Auckland Regional Council in two weeks. We can't simply show up there empty handed."

"Well, that's your problem, not mine," she said, shooting to her feet.

"I quit two days ago, remember."

His eyes flashed with surprise at her flippant words. She could tell he hadn't been expecting that response. Well, gone were the days when she slaved and sacrifice her nights and weekends for Stone. She no longer cared.

"Betty, you told me if I had any questions to give you a call."

She folded her arms across her chest. "And you did call, with your question, and I answered." She shrugged her shoulders. "Well, I don't know'," she said, not even trying to mask the sarcasm in her voice.

She watched as Mark's eyes narrowed to slits, his eyes hardening to tiny chips of blue ice. She could tell by the dark frown on his face that her offhand comment had struck a nerve.

"Betty, what is your problem? I am telling you that I need your Help."

She stiffened at the simmering fury in his eyes, her own gaze turning cold.

"Well, you're CEO now so you don't really need my help," she spit out, realizing how childish she sounded, but she didn't care.

"I already told you I had nothing to do with that," he said gently.

He was right. And when she glimpsed the wounded expression on his face, she instantly felt ashamed of her behavior. It wasn't fair to hold something that was beyond his control against him. She blew out a tired breath.

"I know, and I'm sorry for my comment. But honestly Mark, I have no idea what happened to those files. I really can't help you."

"Can't or won't?" he asked tightly.

"Both," she said quietly, and stepped around him to head toward the door. She froze when his hands clamped around her arms, and he dragged her up against his hard body, her back brushing against his chest.

A tiny shiver raced down her spine when she felt the distinct outline of his cock through her clothing. She instantly pushed out her hips to put some space between their bodies.

"I can't let you walk out of here," he whispered into her ear, and she had to repress a shudder when his warm breath was across her sensitive skin and ears, causing tiny goose bumps to break out across her flesh.

"According to company policy, if an employee quits and anything, from physical property to information, goes missing then I have to report it to the authorities."

"What?" She pulled out of his grasp and turned around to face him, her eyes flashing with disbelief.

"Are you saying you think I took those files?"

"You were angry.

Who could blame you if you wanted to sabotage the company."

She drew back as if he'd struck her, unable to believe his words. "I didn't do anything with those files. When I left Thursday, they were here," she cried, pointing at her computer.

His eyes remained cold, and his expression impassive, as he stared back at her. She could tell from the look on his face that he had his doubts.

"I want to believe you, Betty, but the files have somehow disappeared. I don't want to have you arrested, but I have no choice."

She stiffened as an icy chill crept through her veins. "Arrested?

Mark, I did not take those files."

She could not believe this was happening. She had worked tirelessly for Stone, only to be screwed out of a promotion and now accused of corporate theft.

She had never felt so helpless in her entire life. She held her breath when Mark tilted his head to the side as if he were calculating some mathematical formula silently.

When he abruptly fixed his gaze upon her, she calmed.

"I don't want to see you arrested; all I want is to be ready for that meeting in two weeks. So, I am willing to keep quiet about this if you help me do just that. Help me put together this account in time."

She released a sigh of relief. She had absolutely no desire to spend any time talking with the authorities trying to convince them of her innocence. If he wanted her to help him with the New Zealand account then she could do that, which is exactly what she said.

"I didn't take those files, but I do understand your position. I am willing to assist you with the account," she murmured reluctantly. Hell, she didn't want to do any such thing. But she also didn't feel like going to jail for corporate theft either.

At her words, a smile of relief spread across his handsome face.

"Good" he started but she quickly held up her hand to silence him.

"Before you get excited, you need to understand that this account took me three months to do and many weekends and eighteen-hour days. If you want it ready in two weeks be prepared to spend all your time doing nothing but this."

He folded his arms across his chest and gave her a genuine smile, but she swore she glimpsed a spark of triumph twinkle in his eyes. "Have no worries. I have cleared my calendar to work on nothing else but this.

For the next two weeks, I am all yours."

CHAPTER 3

Teamwork

Mark nearly laughed aloud when Betty signaled at him for several tense seconds as if she was trying to search out the deeper meaning of his words. He could tell the moment she'd brushed his comment aside, as if it was a joke, by the slight shake of her head.

He wanted to grab hold of her and shake her. She was a brilliant woman, but for some reason she always chose to play dumb when it came to his obvious flirting and comments.

He knew she saw the look in his eyes and understood the meaning of his words, and yet she pretended as if she didn't.

"We need to start on this now," he said moving toward the door to her old office. "I will grab an extra chair."

"Oh no. I'm not working here on a Saturday anymore. Again, you forget I am no longer an employee."

She pulled out a notepad from her desk drawer and like two days before she scribbled something down for him. "Here is my address." She handed him the piece of paper and brushed past him to the door.

"Bring all the files and your laptop. We'll work on it there," she said. And without asking him if that was alright, she flung open her old door, walked through and slammed it behind her.

He quirked his lips into a grin, not even the tiniest bit uneasy by her arrogance. This was playing out better than even he could have ever imagined. Betty, in her home, alone, on a Saturday. No, even better, for the next two weeks. It was perfect.

Mark slowed down his black Lexus LS to a crawl and listened to the next instructions from his GPS. He turned his car to the right to make the indicated turn and then picked up speed when he realized he had another half a mile before his next turn.

He glanced around at the spacious grounds of the luxury homes that stretched before him. With a home nestled in the exclusive gated community of Buckhead, he knew Betty lived extremely well.

He turned off Peachtree onto Northside Road and drove for another mile until he pulled up to a uniformed security guard who stood beside a large iron gate.

He handed the guard his license and waited for him to check his name against the Visitor's List. He half expected the guard would hand him back his license and tell him to get lost.

If Betty wanted to, she could have easily returned home, locked herself away and refused to take any of his calls. It wasn't like he could force her to either. He'd lied to her. No, Stone authorities would be banging on her door anytime soon, ever for that matter.

As soon as she'd left her office Thursday, he'd backed up the account on his external hard drive and a CD before erasing her files. The account was still there, not stolen, not lost, just hidden.

He loosened his grip on his steering wheel and relaxed when the guard opened the gate and nodded for him to go through. He pressed his foot down on the accelerator.

Betty had not called his bluff after all. He was in!

It took him just two more minutes to pull into the circular driveway of her large three-story home. The white brick shimmered under the soft rays of the sunlight, as the lush green lawn of her front yard sparkled like a field of shiny emerald.

The exterior of her home was beautiful, warm, and inviting. Much like the owner, although she did her best not to show it.

He piled out of his sedan and grabbed the bag he'd stuffed full of jump drives and manila folders. With the bag slung over his shoulder, he walked to her front door and rang the bell.

He'd barely drawn in full breath when the door opened. She stood there dressed in the same yellow tank top and comfortable fitting ripped jeans she'd worn to the office.

His jaw had dropped when she'd stormed into her old office in unexpected attire. He knew she was in her early forties, but she looked refreshingly vivacious in the hip clothing that was so different from her dull suits, which she only occasionally abandoned for something a little more flamboyant and daring like the dress she'd worn on the day he'd first met her. But again, that was rare. He liked her in her casual outfit.

For one, he could see more of her lush figure as the top scooped down to hug her full breasts and the jeans rode dangerously low on her hips to reveal just the hint of bare skin.

Her hair had been loose when she'd arrived earlier, and he thought she looked beautiful with it down because it framed her lovely face. He was disappointed to see that she'd pulled it back into a ponytail and take off her infamous glasses.

He was certain that if it hadn't been a Saturday, she probably would have changed into a suit just out of habit.

"Here, come in." She stepped aside to let him in before closing the door behind him. That's when he noticed the pale pink polish on her tiny toes. A smile flashed across his face.

Now that was unexpected. Who knew the uptight vice pres. had a softer side after all.

He followed her through the spacious walkway of her home toward her office. He was sure the interior décor was just as lovely as the exterior of her home, but he didn't see any of it because his gaze stayed glued to the lush roundness of her ass that filled out her jeans perfectly.

His eyes snapped to her face just in time to meet her gaze when she abruptly turned around to point to her left. "The bathroom and kitchen are that way. If you need something just help yourself."

Despite the innocence of her words, he was forced to gulp down a deep breath when tingles of pleasure shot straight to his cock. He wanted to help himself to something alright, but it was certainly not down that hallway.

They rounded a sharp corner and walked into a large home office that rivaled her space at work. And like her work office, Betty had everything from a fax machine to a paper shredder tucked away in a neat and tidy fashion. He bit back a grin.

She was just so organized. He wondered what it would take to rumple her feathers and her carefully ordered life.

"You can put everything right there." She gestured to a sturdy glass coffee table on the other side of her desk.

He nodded and began to pull everything from the bag he'd carried inside. Flipping open his laptop, he took a seat on the couch behind the table. He sat there, his lips twisting into a slight frown as he stared back at the computer screen.

He didn't relish the thought of working on an account that technically was already done, but then he glanced across the room and pointed in on the reason why he was there in the first place.

He cracked the knuckles in his fingers and stretched out his hands. This was going to be a rough two weeks of endless work, but he comforted himself with the knowledge that it would be worth it to spend most of it with Betty.

Then, he pushed his cursor across his screen, clicked on the files he needed, and squatted down for a long day of work.

Betty pulled off her glasses and with the same hand stifled a yawn. She glanced at the clock against the wall, 12:13. It was past midnight.

They'd been working for over twelve straight hours, and they hadn't even made a dent in pulling together the account. She reached up and massaged her sore neck, releasing a weary sigh. She couldn't believe she had to spend the next two weeks of her life working on a stupid account she'd finished months ago. It was just so frustrating.

Closing her eyes, she leaned back in her chair, rotating her neck in a slow circle.

"Is your neck sore?"

She snapped her eyelids open and stared back at Matthew, a tiny smile on her face.

"A little," she shrugged, dropping her hand from her neck.

"Here, let me see if I can help," he said, standing to his feet.

Her eyes widened. "Oh, no. You don't have to do that," she said with a dismissive wave of her hand.

A grin tugged at the corners of his lips as he crossed the room in three easy strides.

"It's no problem," he said coming to stop directly behind her.

"Here, let me see," he murmured, his large hands settling against her shoulders.

She blocked the urge to stiffen when his warm palms began to stroke her bare skin. Tiny flickers of heat spread across her back, down her spine and straight to her nipples. She gasped when they suddenly tightened, and she instantly jerked away.

"That's good. It feels better already," she mumbled as she pushed out of her chair to rocket to her feet.

"Are you alright?" he asked, his brows lifting above searching eyes.

"Of course. Thanks for the massage," she hastily murmured, flashing him a weak smile.

He studied her for several moments in silence, his blue gaze intense as he focused solely on her. The examination unnerved her and for some reason she felt nervous.

She moved to step around him but stopped when his arm shot out to block her path.

She glanced down at his arm and then up at his face. At the same time, he lifted his other hand to remove her glasses.

"You know, you have beautiful eyes, but it is hard to tell when you wear these things," he said softly.

She blinked at him for just a moment before she instantly gathered herself together. She didn't know what he was up to, but she was too old for whatever game he was playing.

"Well, at my age it is more important to be able to see than to look good," she said tersely, and held out her hand for her glasses.

He shook his head as if to say he wasn't returning them. "You're not old and I think you look good with or without them beautiful actually."

A curious warmth swirled in her belly, but she pushed it aside. Mark had never shown the slightest interest in her before and now suddenly, he was flirting with her. Well, she wasn't buying it.

"Look Mark, I don't know what you're up to, but as long as we're working."

She stopped when he abruptly reached behind her head and unfastened her hair clip to release her hair so that it fell in soft waves to her shoulders. She was so stunned by his actions that she stood there speechless.

"I also think you look lovely with your hair down. But again, I just prefer you that way. You look beautiful no matter how you wear it."

She took a step back but was forced to stop when she backed into her desk.

Mark was acting so strangely, and she was at a loss. She lifted her hand to press her palm against his chest and almost regretted her actions when she felt the subtle bulge of muscle ripple beneath her hand.

She met his gaze with wide eyes but froze at the look on his face. It was desire?

She had to force herself not to gasp. He was a handsome man, but he was young, too young. And now with the late hour he was probably feeling horny. She blanked that out of her mind. She didn't know what it was he was feeling but she did know that he needed to take his strange behavior and go.

"It's getting late and I'm tired. I think it's time for you to go."

Desperately needing to put some space between them, she moved to duck around him, but didn't manage to get far when his arm snaked around her waist and he dragged her up against his body.

Her eyes rounded and she flattened her hands against his chest to push him away. "What are you doing?"

She should have known from the devilish gleam in his eyes that he was up to something, but when he dipped his head to press his lips against hers, there was no longer any doubt.

She gasped in surprise as she stood there frozen, but that was big mistake.

As soon as she parted her lips, he swept inside, his tongue teasing the moist flesh of her mouth as he stroked it around, coaxing her to surrender. He didn't have to wait long. Shocks of warm pleasure skated across her skin and warmth pooled at her hot center as every nerve in her body crackled with energy.

She closed her eyes, twisted her arms behind his neck and simply melted against him as her body disintegrated into one big mass of jelly. Wet heat gushed from inside her to dampen her panties when he cupped her ass and drew her closer to the temptation of his lengthening cock.

A sigh of pleasure tore past her lips and she rocked her hips against him, causing him to grow harder against her belly.

Lost so deep in the ecstasy of his kiss, it took her a second to realize he'd unfastened her jeans and was already tugging down the zipper.

From somewhere deep inside of her she tapped into that buried well of reserve willpower and found the strength to wrench her lips from his and push him away.

His face was flushed as he stood there panting. She was sure she looked pretty much the same. Even now her lips still tingled with the taste of him.

"You need to go," she rasped out breathlessly, but her tone was firm.

He opened his mouth to protest, but instantly closed it, apparently glimpsing the determined look in her eyes. He dipped his head in a slight nod, seeming to accept her words. But he didn't move as a lopsided grin slowly spread across his face.

"I never even thought to ask you this before I kissed you, but are you single?" he said sheepishly.

She coughed nervously as her gaze dotted around the room, landing on everything but him. "Um, I don't see how that is important."

He wrinkled his forehead as he frowned, ignoring her flippant brush off. "It's very important to me. I need to know if you are taken before I invest any more time in this and possibly make a fool of myself if I haven't already."

She drew back slightly, her hands curling into fists against her hips as her eyes began to simmer with fury.

"Invest more time in this? You make it sound like it's a chore. I guess you're referring to getting to know me, or something, but for the record you haven't invested any time in doing that. And that kiss certainly doesn't count," she snapped.

Was she crazy? He'd been trying to get to know her for two years! His nostrils flared and his own temper began to take root. He knew it wasn't wise to argue with the woman you were actively courting or trying to, but he chalked his stupidity up to sleep removal.

"Getting to know you is all I've been trying to do from the day I met you, but woman you are a hard person to get to know. With your Cold Bitch routine, it has been virtually impossible, no, make that completely impossible."

Mark instantly regretted his harsh words when a wounded look flashed in her eyes. He opened his mouth to apologize but never got the chance when her pained expression immediately disappeared and was replaced by the cold, hard woman he was so used to seeing every day at work.

"If I'm such a bitch then why you would even want to get to know me? And besides, did you ever once consider that this Cold Bitch routine isn't a routine at all.

I know it may be hard for you to believe, but maybe I'm not interested in getting to know you," she shot back.

He gritted his teeth together, before closing the distance between them, to grasp her by the arms and drag her flush against his muscled frame, ignoring her shocked expression.

"I know what you're doing but it won't work. It would be so easy for you to push me away and have me walk out that door. You probably do that with a lot of men, and it works."

"That's ridiculous. Now let go of me."

"I just want to know if you're available Betty because I want the chance to get to know you better."

Her eyes grew wider if that was even possible. "A chance?

Mark, I am almost twice your age. Even if I wanted to, I wouldn't even entertain the idea. You are far too young for me."

He wanted to shake her. She wasn't even close to being twice his age. Still, their age difference was the obvious obstacle for her, and he knew that she would use that as her first excuse. He also knew what some of the others would be so he laid them on the table before she could throw them up in his face.

"I guess I'm too white for you too. I know that's your next excuse.

If you hadn't quit, you could have used the fact that I was your new boss as a good one.

I think that one would have had some merit," he mocked. "What else? Am I too tall? Too inexperienced?"

"I get it okay," she bit out. "Mark, this is ridiculous."

"What is ridiculous about wanting to get to know you?"

She must have heard the soft plea in his voice because the fire seemed to go out of her, and her brown eyes instantly softened. She shook her head. "Nothing, I guess," she said quietly.

"I'm very flattered that you're interested in getting to know me, but you are a very young man, and I am sure there are plenty of women your age that would suit you better."

His fingers tightened around her arms as he struggled not to let his irritation with her show on his face. Hadn't they just gone over this? He didn't need a lecture from her about their age difference.

"I'm sure there are a lot of women that would suit me just fine, but that has nothing to do with the question I asked you," he bit out. "Are you single Betty, yes or no," he repeated when she parted her lips to resume her protest.

"Yes, I'm single."

"Great. That's all I needed to know."

CHAPTER 4

The Intruder

"Shit." Betty scowled at her computer screen when she realized she'd spent the last five minutes inputting the wrong data into the wrong column of her Excel spreadsheet. She jerked off her glasses and pinched the bridge of her nose.

The events from the night before kept playing in her head like a broken record. Not only had she admitted to Mark that she was available but then she'd promised to go out on a date with him as soon as he returned from New Zealand in three weeks.

He wanted to take her out sooner, but she'd reminded him that if they were going to finish the account in time for his trip to New Zealand that they just didn't have the time to spare.

He'd seen the wisdom of her advice and agreed, although very reluctantly, but not before she promised to give him a rain check.

"What is wrong with you? How did you allow a twenty-nine-year-old to browbeat you into a date of all things?"

She shook her head at the absurdity of the situation. He was a handsome, manly, wealthy man. There had to be an endless line of beauties trying to break down his door. "So, what the hell does he want with me?" She muttered aloud.

At forty-one she held no illusions about her shortcomings. She did her best to eat healthy, exercise and take care of herself, but she was not under any naïve impression that her full breasts were still perky and that there weren't visible pockets of cellulite in places where she wished they weren't. She frowned at that thought.

Mark undoubtedly had his pick of women, so why her?

The doorbell chimed, interrupting her thoughts, and she glanced at her clock in the corner of her computer. Speak of the devil. Mark was right on time.

On bare feet, she padded down the hall to the front door and pulled it open. He stood there looking breathtakingly handsome with his dark hair combed back off his face wearing a white polo shirt and khaki pants that fit him perfectly.

Her heartbeat faster in her chest as she stood to the side to let him in, the scent of his aftershave tickling her nose when he brushed past.

"Hi. You ready to get to work?" She asked, wondering if that breathy, husky voice she'd just heard was really hers.

"Yep," he said with a heart-stopping grin, and she had to mentally shake herself to keep from drowning in the twin blue pools of his eyes.

"What?" She asked when he stood there staring at her with a puzzled look on his face. That's when she noticed there was a bouquet of flowers in his outstretched hand.

"Mark," "I can't believe you want to argue with me about this. They're a Gift for you." He held out his hand again. "Take them," he said softly.

Not wanting to seem childish by protesting over something as innocent as flowers, she grasped the bouquet of pink roses as she smiled.

"Thank you."

His face seemed to light up when he grinned down at her and in that moment, something clicked inside her. He seemed genuine in his interest in her. She could tell by the way he looked at her that seeing her happy, seemed to make him happy.

She gave a mental shrug as she accepted that he had a simple crush on her. She could handle that. Hell, there were worse things than having the harmless attention of a handsome young man.

Her smile grew wider when he tugged her into his arms, but unlike last night she didn't protest. "What are you doing?" She asked, although she already knew.

His eyes twinkled with mischief.

"Nothing right now, but I'm getting ready to kiss you since I've softened you up with the flowers."

"Ah, I see, your little Trojan Horse," she chuckled softly, before she closed her eyes and tipped her head back to meet his warm lips. He kissed her sweetly, as he took his time exploring her mouth with his tongue.

He slowly built a fire inside her and then as he deepened the kiss, he fanned the flames until she was feverish. With her free hand, she clung to him, as their lips and bodies fused together.

It was a long time before they pulled away from each other.

"Mmmm, you make it hard for a man to want to concentrate on work."

She laughed softly as she moved away from him to walk back down her hallway.

"Well, you better concentrate or else you will lose the New Zealand account and that is no way to start off as CEO."

He twisted his lips into a surly frown, and she bit her cheek to keep from laughing.

At that moment, he looked like a little boy, but she knew he wouldn't appreciate her saying that.

"You certainly know how to cool a man's enthusiasm too," he grumbled.

She flashed him a wicked grin.

"They don't call me the Cold Bitch for nothing," she quipped from over her shoulder, before she turned her head around and headed into her office, where they both settled in for another grueling day of work.

Betty stretched her arms above her head and yawned.

"I'm calling it a night," she mumbled weakly past another yawn as she swiveled her chair around to face Mark.

As soon as she saw him, she couldn't help but smile. His mouth was slightly open, as his head rested against the back of her small couch. He was fast asleep.

She crossed the room to remove the laptop that still sat on his legs.

She saved all his files and closed it up, before flipping the lights off in her office.

It was close to two in the morning. No sense in waking him just so he could drive home sleepy. She turned off all the lights on the first level, except for the one in the hallway that led to the bathroom just in case he wakes up in the middle of the night.

She then set the house alarm and climbed the stairs to her own bedroom.

As soon as she closed the bedroom door behind her, she quickly removed her jeans and black t-shirt to put on a nightgown, before collapsing across her bed in exhaustion.

In minutes she too was fast asleep.

The sharp sound of something breaking apart instantly startled him, waking him up. He blinked for several seconds until his eyes adjusted to the darkness. It took him another few moments to remember where he was.

When his foggy mind began to clear he instantly became alert. Betty.

He shot off the couch and crept around the corner. He squinted his eyes against the brightness of the light from the hallway but was grateful for it because it gave him a clear path to the stairs that led up to the second floor where she slept.

The creaking of a door startled him, and he bounded up the stairs, two at a time, his fear for Lana dogging his steps. When he reached the second floor he struggled to adjust to the darkness once again.

As soon as he did, he saw from the corner of his eyes a shadowy figure moving slowly. With silent steps he crept in that direction.

His sneakers dug into the plush carpet, muffling each step he took, as he silently stalked the figure moving away from him. He frowned.

He didn't know which of the four rooms upstairs was Betty's, but he wondered if the intruder was someone he knew and if he was headed straight to her bedroom.

He quickened his pace until he stood at the foot of the intruder.

Lunging forward, he tackled him to the ground at the same time the Intruder turned around.

Mark's eyes widened when he realized his error, but it was already too late.

"Ahhhh," Betty cried as she tumbled beneath the weight of a heavy object and her back crashed to the floor. Terror instantly gripped her, and she lashed out with her fists. She landed several blows before she realized the muffled voice calling her name was familiar.

"Mark?"

There was a low grumble and then the heavy weight rolled off her. She dragged a deep breath of air into her lungs, since most of it had been knocked out of her when she fell, and then stood to her feet to flip the light on in the hallway.

"Oh my God," she cried when she saw that Mark now stood on his feet, clutching a small purple bruise just beneath his right eye. "Are you alright?"

He winced slightly as he nodded. "I'll be fine. Are you alright? I heard a noise."

"Yeah, me too, but I think maybe the wind just knocked over a flowerpot or something." She drew closer to him and reached up to remove his hand from his face.

She hissed when she saw the bruise was now darker and had started to swell. "I'm sorry. I thought you were an intruder. Here, let me get you some ice for that," she said, ushering him down the stairs toward the kitchen.

He sat down on a barstool on the other side of her breakfast counter while she wrapped some ice cubes in a towel.

"How's your back?" he asked when she came around to press the ice pack against his face. "Ah." He instantly jerked away when it touched his skin.

"I'm so sorry." she said, her lips bowing into a deep frown. "And my back is fine. Thank you."

She pressed the ice pack against his skin again, this time her actions were calmer, and he didn't flinch.

He lifted his hand and curled it around hers, holding the ice against his eye.

At the touch of his fingers against her skin, her gaze snapped to his face, as a sharp current of electricity passed between them, sending sizzling heat spreading across her body.

She slowly registered that she stood there in a white satin night gown that molded every curve of her body.

As if reading her mind, his gaze dipped lower to stay on her now stiff nipples, before drifting lower, igniting a simmering fire within her as he openly devoured her with his gaze.

She tried to pull away, but couldn't when he wrapped his arm around her waist and dragged her between his legs.

"Mark?" she gasped breathlessly.

A devilish look twinkled in his eyes, but it did not hide the lust that burned like a fire in his blue gaze.

Her heart pumped wildly in her chest, and she sucked in a breath to try to still her now trembling body.

He forced the ice pack from her boneless fingers and placed it on the countertop. Before she knew what he was doing he stood at his feet, gripped the back of her head, and lowered his mouth to her parted lips.

Her eyes widened and she stared at him for several shocked moments before she too let her eyes drift shut. With nothing left to do but focus on his kiss she wrapped her arms behind his neck and melted against him.

He groaned into her mouth; at the same time, he slipped his tongue between her lips. Electricity sizzled down her spine and she tangled her hands into his hair, gripping him closer.

Warning bells dinged in her head telling her this was all kinds of wrong, but she ignored them as her body hummed to life. Heat pooled at the center of her core as she felt the sticky wetness begin to seep from inside her.

A low moan escaped her lips, and she deepened the kiss to intertwine her tongue with his. Heated radiated off his chiseled body to inflame her skin and she swore she would go up in flames right there.

God, she wanted him. She hadn't even realized how much until now. Yet when she felt the press of his engorged length against her belly, she experienced a moment's hesitation. The realization of where this was headed was like a bucket of cold water being thrown over her head.

Despite the protests of her aching body, she slid her hands from his neck and wrenched her mouth from his.

He stood there wide eyed and panting, his face flushed. He looked wild, untamed, a virile man in his prime, and she knew that's what made him so dangerous.

"We better get to bed. I mean not together. You know.

Separately," she paused out nervously. Betty wanted to smack herself. She sounded like a dumb teenage girl experiencing her first crush. She felt even more foolish when Mark stared down at her with a knowing grin.

With his arm still locked around her waist, he pulled her closer and slid the thumb of his free hand across her full bottom lip.

Against her will, her body shuddered, and she nearly melted from embarrassment when his grin grew wider.

"I make you nervous, don't I?"

He did, but she wasn't going to admit that to him. She was a grown woman. Even though he was almost thirty, to her, he was barely legal. How would it look to admit that a kid, practically half her age, made her nervous?"

"No, of course not," she blurted out quickly, just a little too quickly. "You're lying," he said softly and to prove his point he slid his thumb across her upper lip this time, and as if on cue she shivered again.

"Your attraction to me makes you nervous." He dipped his head to her neck, brushing his lips against her skin, before snagging the spaghetti strap of her gown with his teeth, to drag it until it fell from her shoulder, revealing the upper swell of her right breast.

"To be honest, you make me nervous too, but in a good way."

A shocked gasp escaped her lips at the same time he traced a path of kisses along her neck all the way down to the top of her breast. She wasn't sure if it was his kisses or the revelation that shocked her, probably both.

"Christ, I want you," he murmured against her skin. "I've wanted you from the day I first met you," he whispered as he skimmed his hand up her body to tug the other strap down.

She struggled to wrap her mind around his words. She had always been polite, but aloof in her dealings with him, and yet he claimed he'd harbored an attraction to her for two years. The sincerity of his declaration boosted her confidence, but she still could not shake the slight doubt that nagged her.

"M," she rasped out when he moved to push her gown down her body. She shook her head and clutched the thin material at her breasts just before it could slip to the floor. She swallowed hard and forced herself to meet his searching gaze.

"I," she struggled to say the words. She was a tough as nails corporate exec. That was how he knew her, how everyone did. How could she admit to him that at the core she was just like any other woman, and that she too had her own insecurities?

"Betty, what is it?"

She dropped her gaze to the floor, as she worried her bottom lip between her teeth.

"I'm not twenty-nine, Mark," she said in a jumbled rush, her eyes still glued to the floor.

She dragged her gaze to his face when he didn't speak, an inward groan welled up inside her when she glimpsed his look of confusion.

God, did she really have to spell it out? "My body. I'm not twenty-nine," she snapped in frustration.

She felt like such a fool for having to say it aloud, even more so when comprehension dawned on his face. She tried to pull out of his arms but couldn't when his hands closed over her tightly curled fists that held the gown to her body like it was a shield.

"I know how old you are, Betty" he said softly as he pried her fingers, one by one until finally the soft satin pooled at her feet.

She moved to cover her naked figure with her arms, but Mark immediately seized her wrists, effectively trapping her arms behind her back.

With her wrists behind her back, her full breasts jutted forward and his eyes zeroed in on their stiffened peaks. "God, you're beautiful," he said hoarsely as he slid his gaze slowly down the length of her body and back up again.

A slight thrill of pleasure shot through her at the look on his face. He appeared to be sincere in his appreciation of what she knew was her damaged figure.

For a moment she still questioned what the hell she was doing, but before she could give her doubts any merit, he released her wrists, backed her up against the breakfast counter and seized her lips in another mind-numbing kiss.

This time the press of his lips was more urgent, demanding even.

He reached behind her to cut the full globes of her ass in his large hands, dragging her flush against his hard body. A moan escaped her lips, and she wrapped her hands behind his head to tangle in his hair.

Now she had her Rabbit, and it did the job, but it had been a long time since a man had made love to her and her body was on fire. Her pussy clenched and unclenched with tiny spasms as if begging for Mark's dick.

She moaned again when Mark dipped his head lower to capture a single nipple between his lips and tugged gently. A fresh wave of moisture gushed from her pussy, and she had to clench her thighs together to keep the juices from trickling down her legs.

"Jesus, Betty you have beautiful tits." He groaned against her breasts which he'd pushed together to flick his tongue across the large, dark nipples.

Her head fell back, and she tightened her hands in his hair as he alternated between each breast to abundant attention on her sensitive nipples, with loud sucking noises. Back and forth he tugged, sucked, and stroked her nipples with his tongue until they were glistening wet.

When he nipped lightly at one tender peak, she nearly collapsed as a bolt of pleasure shot straight to her aching cunt.

"Mark, please. I—I need you inside me," she begged, her nails digging into his scalp.

"You are just so gorgeous. I love your tits. I could play with them forever," he said between kisses as he reluctantly released her breasts to trace a path down her stomach.

He stayed at her belly button to slip his tongue inside the groove, and she jerked in surprise. "I fantasized about this moment for so long. I knew your body would burn for me as soon as I touched it," he whispered at the same time he dragged a single finger between her moist folds.

He lifted his head to meet her gaze and with his eyes fixed solely on her he sucked his finger between his lips to taste her cream. She gasped at the look of pleasure on his face before he closed his eyes and moaned.

"You taste so good, so sweet. I need more," he said softly and tugged her down to the kitchen floor.

In one fluid movement, he pushed her heels back against her butt, spread her thighs and lowered his face between her legs.

At the first touch of his tongue against her sex she arched her back off the floor, liquid heat pumping though her veins.

"Mark," she cried out. Her body quivering as pleasure zoomed straight to where his mouth nibbled on her tiny nub.

He pushed a single finger inside her as he sucked hard on her clit, dragging hoarse moans from her lips.

He quickened his pace, pumping his finger in and out of her until her juices poured from her cunt. "Yes, yes, yes," she moaned wildly as she struggled against the floor.

He consumed her pussy with his mouth, while the finger fucked her hard. She spread her legs wider and tugged wildly at his hair. She was so, so close.

She clenched her eyes shut, her head rolling back as her orgasm rocketed through her, forcing a sharp cry from her lips "That's it. Come for me Betty. Come all over my face," he groaned against her pussy and what little control she had left completely shattered at his words.

She closed her thighs against his head and screamed his name over and over, her body shaking with each tremor that coursed through her.

"Mark," she moaned out as her climax slowly began to subside, tiny quakes shooting though her limp body. She loosened her grip on his head to tunnel her fingers through his soft hair, tousling it in several directions. She opened her eyes to watch him lap up her cum and almost came again at the erotic image of him eating her out.

"Mumm, I enjoyed that."

Finally satisfied, he slid up the length of her body, to cover her with his large, chiseled frame.

"Me, too," she murmured as she seized the bottom of his shirt with her hands and worked to pull it over his head.

"But I need more."

He shrugged out of his shirt with a grin on his face. "What? That wasn't enough?" He teased, as he unzipped his pants.

"Oh, it was more than enough, but I guess I need something different now. Something bigger, harder."

The words came out on a hoarse whisper as she slipped her hand inside his pants, curling them around his stiff erection.

Heat curled in her belly at the realization that her hand could not fit around his thickness. She pulled his dick from inside his pants as he pushed them down his hips. Her eyes widened at his size. He was both thick and long. In a word perfect.

Their eyes met and her heart slammed into her chest. As if on cue, her pussy started to spasm and moisture seeped from her slit. She lightly pumped his cock in her hand until it jerked between her fingers.

She glanced down at the purple head of his dick and knew they were well past the point of foreplay.

"Do you have protection?"

He nodded and kicked off his pants to dig out a small foil packet from his wallet. While he sheathed himself, she studied him. From the way he filled out his suits, she knew he would be impressively built, and she was right, as the muscles in his large arms flexed with each motion it took to slide on the condom.

As she raked her gaze over the chiseled definition of his muscled frame, she experienced a moment's hesitation. What was she doing sleeping with him? He was so unbelievably young.

She probably would have backed out of it had he not grabbed the back of her head and dragged her against him, to kiss her deeply. She wondered briefly if he did that on purpose. Kiss her to distraction.

She opened her mouth and welcomed his interested tongue, moaning at the taste of herself on his lips. She leaned back then as he settled his weight over her body, parting her legs to cushion him between her thighs. He tore his lips from hers at the same time he positioned himself at her opening.

"I want to see your face when I enter you for the first time," he said in answer to the questioning look she shot him when he broke their kiss.

She nodded slowly, lifting her hands to caress his back. She swore she would hold his intense gaze when he entered her, but as he pushed inside her cunt, stretching her inner walls, he stroked against her g-spot, and she shattered again.

CHAPTER 5

One Night Stand

Oh God,," he rasped from above her when she came again, her pussy grabbing him like a tight fist as it coated his dick with her warm juices.

He didn't move a muscle as she screamed out her orgasm, her body clenching and unclenching around his engorged length. He couldn't move if he wanted to, her grip was so tight, but he also didn't dare, for fear that he would spill his seed without so much as a second thrust inside her tight sheath.

"Wrap your legs around my waist," he croaked out when the tremors that racked her started to subside. She did, at the same time twisting her arms behind his back, clinging to him. He lowered himself against her, gripped her ass in his hands and slowly began to ride her.

She was beautiful, soft, and lush like a woman should be. Her thick thighs cushioned him as he pumped his hips back and forth to tunnel inside her. A deep groan fell from his lips, and he closed his eyes to just savor the feel of the soft pillow of her breasts against his chest. Her body was luxurious and feminine, a modern-day Venus.

She'd made a point to tell him she didn't have the body of a twenty-nine-year-old. He'd wanted to tell her then that he couldn't have cared less about that; it was her that he wanted.

She had the body of a woman, who didn't pick over everything she ate. That was unbelievably sexy to him a woman with curves that he could hold on to when he made love to her.

If proving his point, he dug his fingers into the soft flesh of her ass and thrust deeper, burying his length in her tight, wet heat.

Her nails wrinkled deeper into his back, but he ignored the slight twinge of pain. Instead, he clenched his lids tighter to crush off his coming climax.

"Mark, that's it. Fuck me harder," she screamed as she threw her hips at him, meeting him thrust for thrust so that his balls slapped loudly against her skin.

Pleasure exploded inside of him, and he lost it. Lifting himself off her, he opened her legs from behind his back, hooked his arms behind her knees and shifted above her. Spreading her wider, he rode her harder.

"Yes, Mark. Fuck me," she screamed, louder this time.

"God, Betty, I'm about to come," he mumbled loudly as he pounded his cock deep inside her pussy. Sweat dripped from his body with each rough thrust as he shoved his dick harder into her tender flesh.

She was just so tight, so wet, and the muscles in his arms bulged as he pushed her legs wider, seemingly unable to get deep enough inside her.

He pumped his hips furiously, his cock pistoning in and out of her at a frenzied pace. When her cunt began to pulse around him again, his control completely snapped, and he shattered. With one final thrust his cock jerked wildly and he exploded.

"Bettyyyyyy," he roared as he emptied his seed inside of her at the same time she came again, her pussy clamping around his dick, milking him of every drop of cum.

He unhooked her legs and collapsed against her, panting heavily. He lay on top of her for several moments, while she stroked her hands across his sweat drenched back. He lifted his lips into a satisfied smile when he heard her purr softly.

Mindful of his heavy weight, he slipped out of her and rolled to her side. He reached for her to pull her against him but calmed. At the same time, he felt her stiffen beside him. The blood immediately froze in his veins.

Their eyes met and he knew that his stunned expression mirrored hers. He swore under his breath when he tried to reach for her, but she pulled away from him.

"Betty, it's going to be okay. I haven't been with a woman in over a year and I always use protection and get tested regularly. I'm good. I swear," he said, hastily tugging off the broken condom.

Her expression was suspicious as she stared at him. "You're good? Well, I'm not," she snapped.

He stiffened. "When was the last time you got tested?" He asked nervously.

She shot him a hard look. "I didn't mean that," she said, her hand waving wildly in the air. "I always use condoms and I get tested regularly too. My last results were fine. I meant that I'm not on birth control."

He blew out a deep breath as relief washed over him. "That's it?"

He stopped when he saw her furious expression. "I meant that we can…."

"We? You mean me." She jumped to her feet, hurriedly to take off her gown.

He sighed again and followed suit by dragging on his pants and shirt. "No, I meant we," he said firmly.

She stared up at him, her expression full of horror, before she dropped her face into her hands and sighed. "This is a nightmare. I knew this was a mistake."

He glared angrily at her; his jaw clenched tight. "What we shared wasn't a mistake, and this certainly isn't a nightmare," he bit out stiffly.

"I want children, so unless you don't, then we can work through this, together."

She dropped her hands to stare at him as if he'd lost his mind. "This is not about wanting children. I want children too, but under the right circumstances.

I certainly don't like the idea of getting pregnant from a one-night stand."

Mark drew in a long breath, silently counting to ten to limit himself from reaching out and shaking her until she started speaking with some sense. Her words were insulting, and he struggled to harness in his mounting fury toward her.

"That's your problem, Betty. Everything must be done your way, by your plan and to your standards. So, you could be pregnant, and we're not married. So what? We'll figure this out. It's not the end of the world."

He knew that as soon as she crossed her arms over her chest and rolled her eyes that he was going to hate her words even more than the ones she'd just spoken. "Not married? Try not even in a relationship?

You're still in your twenties. To you this seems so simple. I get pregnant, we have a baby, and we just take care of it."

He scowled at the mocking tone of her voice, the sound grating on his ears, but he forced himself to bite down on his tongue to keep from lashing out in anger.

"Well, it's not that simple. Not for me, and if you were more mature you would realize not for you either."

"So, I'm immature now?" He snorted rudely. Unable to look at her any longer, he spun away from her and stalked off in the direction of her office. He couldn't believe how unreasonable she was being.

He quickly gathered his things and nearly bowled her over when he turned around and she was standing there, blocking his path.

"What are you doing?"

"I'm leaving. I think you need some time alone to figure out why our age difference is such a problem for you, because it isn't for me." He shook his head, not even trying to hide his disappointment.

"The sad thing is that it never even entered my mind to call what we just shared a one night stand, but those were your first thoughts. Just as the idea that you're pregnant is not a bad thing in my eyes, but you can only see it is as a nightmare."

He shot her a defeating look when she opened her mouth to argue. He'd had enough of her important words, unintentional they might have been, for one night.

"Like I said, I think you need some time alone to come to the realization that I am a mature man, who is quite capable of being a responsible father," he said quietly and stepped around her before she could say another word.

As he slipped silently from her home, he hoped she would think over his words that night. The attraction between them was not one-sided and he needed her to come to terms with that before they went any further, or else she was never going to take him seriously.

CHAPTER 6

Robing the Cradle

Betty pulled her ruby red convertible Ferrari into her reserved parking spot and flipped the ignition to off. She hadn't submitted an official letter of resignation, so her spot was empty, since technically it was still hers.

She'd planned to give her notice today, but all that had changed when Mark stormed from her home in a fit last night.

She dragged in a ragged breath as she gripped the steering wheel. "What did I do?" She asked herself what must have been the hundredth time. Long after Mark's departure, she'd tossed and turned, unable to sleep.

At first, memories of their lovemaking had kept her up. The sex had been explosive and shocking.

She'd had her share of lovers in the past, enough to know that her experience with Mark had been special.

"Shit. That stupid word again," she hissed out, hating that it kept creeping back into her thoughts whenever she thought of him, which was every waking moment.

When she wasn't thinking of him and the amazing sex, then there were his words which he'd spoken before he'd stormed out.

Yes, he was young, but he was a full-grown man. He'd never done anything in the time she'd known him to suggest that he was irresponsible or immature.

"But he's just so young," she cried. What would her friends think? She bounced her forehead against the steering wheel three times.

They would think she was a desperate cradle robber cougar who'd been so jumped off the sex that she'd been foolish enough to get herself knocked up by her boy lover.

"Hell, if it wasn't me, that's what I would think," she muttered dryly and checked her reflection in the mirror on her visor.

"Ugh," she mumbled in disgust as she stared at her haggard expression. It was guilt, plain and simple. No matter that she had been less the seductress and more the seduced, she'd lain awake all night because she was too old to be sleeping with Mark and should have had sense enough to stop things before, they'd gotten out of hand.

She hadn't. Quite the opposite. She'd practically flung herself headfirst into a low affair.

"Now, you could be pregnant, you dummy," she punished herself because as soon as Mark left, she'd raced upstairs to check her calendar, and based upon her calculations, she sat somewhere between a miracle and a prayer.

She banged her head against the steering wheel three more times for good measure. "Just so stupid, stupid, stupid."

She sat there alone in her car for several more minutes until she felt strong enough to gather her things and make the short walk inside.

She knew Mark had an early morning meeting and decided to head him off before he got any ideas about showing up at her door to finish the account.

As angry as he'd been, she'd doubted he would even return, but when she remembered that he had to finish the account, she concluded he really had no other choice, but she did.

What had seemed like a good idea to work on the account from the comfort of her home, had backfired. So now she was back at the office for the next two weeks.

No way they could slip up again if they were at the very busy, very occupied office. At least that's what she hoped.

Mark scowled at his computer screen as he sat back in his chair to rub his hand across the scratchy beard along his jaw.

She thought she was so clever coming into the office. She thought it would be easier to keep him at arm's length if they were in the safety of their office. She was wrong.

He glanced at the clock. Ten p.m. They'd been there all day, working on the accounts, shuttling back and forth between their offices with questions, both professional and polite.

Both pretending as if nothing had changed, but everything had changed.

He shrugged out of his suit jacket and removed his tie. What was he doing? Here he was working on an account that was already done to woo a woman who was as stubborn as a mule.

This was not working out at all how he planned.

"That's because you didn't plan, you idiot. You just acted," he grumbled in frustration.

Like an immature, spoiled, fool, he wanted to add, but figured idiot was enough.

Now, because of his impulsive actions, Betty could well in fact be pregnant. As a result, she was barely speaking to him.

He'd spoken the truth last night. He wanted children, and he was fine with having them now. Granted, he would have liked to have waited a couple of years so he could scale back his hours at work.

His father had been a workaholic who was rarely around when he was growing up so he'd sworn to himself that when he had kids, he would be there for them.

As he'd told Betty last night, they would figure things out together. He refused to let work interfere with the raising of his child. Between the two of them, Betty was the true workaholic.

Yet somewhere deep down, he sensed having a child would change that.

Leaning back in his chair, he closed his eyes as he imagined Betty as a mother, and smiled at the thought of seeing her belly swell with his child and how an active toddler would be just what she needed to upset her carefully ordered life.

He knew she would make an excellent mother, patient, attentive, and loving. The sound of his office door slamming shut shook him from his fantasy and his eyes snapped open to see the very object of his thoughts, standing before him with her hands on her hips, wearing a frown across her face.

"I can't believe you've fallen asleep again. I was just about to tell you that I was going to go, thinking you were hard at work." She stalked across the room to stand behind him and stare at his computer. "How far have you even gotten?"

He swiveled his chair around, throwing her off balance so that he had to follow her hips to steady her before she fell across him.

"I just closed my eyes for a second. Besides, I've been working on this for eleven hours straight. Even if I haven't gotten as far as you would have liked, I'm done for the night too."

She narrowed her eyes at his slight reprimand. "Fine, well good night then," she said tightly and planted her feet so that she could stand up straight.

"You can let go of me now. I'm not going to fall." She frowned when his hands remained at her hips.

In one fluid motion he stood at his feet, leaned back against his desk, and pulled her up against him. When she struggled against him, he swung her around and pinned her between him and the desk.

"Mark," she said on a weary sigh, her face twisting into a scowl.

"I thought we understood each other. Last night was a onetime thing, never to happen again."

He leaned forward, burying his face in her neck. "I understood no such thing."

She pushed against his chest. "Mark, I'm serious."

"I am too," he said in a husky whisper, and lifted her up to sit her on top of his desk.

Stepping between her legs he slid his hands under her skirt, along her thighs. His cock, which had stood at attention the minute she walked in, grew rock hard when his hands stroked the bare skin of her lush ass.

Lacy thigh highs and a thong. "Sexy," he groaned against her neck, in between the tiny kisses he placed along her throat where her black blouse was open. She'd loosened two buttons, but he planned to undo them all.

"Stop it, Mark," she demanded on a harsh whisper, and he chuckled softly when instead of pushing against his chest, her hands fisted into the fabric of his dress shirt.

"You don't want me to stop, and you know it." He reluctantly skimmed his hands back down her thighs and reached up to push her dress jacket down her arms. He quickly tossed it aside.

Then, he undid the buttons of her blouse, sending the shirt flying across the room as soon as he got it off her. Not bothering to unclasp her bra, he simply tugged the straps down so that her heavy breasts tumbled from the black, lacy cups.

"Did you lie awake last night recalling how good it felt when I slid inside you?" He grinned when a breathless moan erupted from her lips.

"I know I did. I thought of you all night and how good your tight cunt felt milking my dick when you came."

"Mark," she said sharply.

He glanced at her and smiled. She stared at him with lust filled eyes, her lips drawn into a sexy wry face. He knew from her expression that she too had thought about how good it had been between them the night before.

"I could barely concentrate today; my thoughts of you were so all consuming." He captured her lips in a slow kiss and gently massaged her breasts in his hands, teasing the nipples to hardened peaks.

He squashed her breasts together and lowered his head to suck her nipples. Sharp tingles of pleasure slid over his body at the sound of her throaty moans, and he sucked harder.

After bathing her nipples until they glistened under the muted light, he lifted his gaze to watch her.

She was just so sexy, with her head thrown back, her mouth open, and her cheeks flushed a dusky rose.

He released her breasts and slid up her body, sticking one hand under her skirt which was now practically bunched up at her hips, to dip a single finger inside of her.

They both sucked in a breath simultaneously. She was dripping wet.

He pushed her thong to the side, and with one handheld it firmly in place, while he undid his pants and slipped his aching cock out with the other.

Gripping his enlarged flesh within his palm, he positioned the head of his dick at the tight, wet opening of her hot cunt and pressed forward until the head slipped inside.

"Mark. No," he heard the alarm in her voice and stopped. He dragged in a shaky breath to tamp down his lust long enough for him to speak.

He met her anxious gaze. "What is it, babe?"

"We need protection."

He grinned sheepishly. "That didn't work so well for us last time."

Her eyes rounded. "You think this is funny, but I'm serious. I could really be pregnant."

"Then we don't need a condom."

Her eyes grew wider. "Mark!"

He let out a sigh and leaned his forehead against hers. "I don't have one honey, and if you could be pregnant then we don't need one."

"But what if I'm not?"

He quirked his lips into a lopsided grin. "Then we should try until you are."

She shot him a fierce look. "That's not funny, Mark."

He traced a trail of kisses across her forehead, down her cheek and along her ear, where he whispered.

"I'm not joking." He dipped his head lower and kissed the hollow space between her collar bone and neck.

"I hope our first child is a girl." He murmured as he shifted his hips so his cock sank deeper inside her moist heat. "Who looks just like you," he groaned against her neck and fed her another slow inch of his stiff erection.

"Mark," she gasped, and he couldn't tell if it was a warning or not.

"If you want me to stop then I will," he whispered softly. "I would never want to do anything that you're not comfortable with."

He pushed forward to ease deeper inside her tight covering. "I would never do anything to hurt you."

He paused to flick his tongue out and trace lazy circles against her soft skin but stopped abruptly when her pussy tightened around him. He closed his eyes and let out a groan as a shudder of pleasure rocked his body.

"God, Betty, you can't tell me that if you feel half as strongly as I do that deep down the thought of having my child doesn't excite you just a little.

Having me bare inside you doesn't turn you on just a little. That the feel of me coming inside you doesn't make you hot, because it sure as hell is making mc hot for you.

Damn, Betty, I think I'm going to burn up just thinking about having your bare pussy wrapped around my dick."

When several moments marked by in silence, he finally lifted his head to meet her gaze.

Confusion and uncertainty shimmered in her eyes, and he was sure that she would deny his words and push him away.

Instead, she reached up to snake one arm behind his neck and pulled him closer to press her lips against his. Her kiss was demanding, and he abandoned himself to the lush taste of her mouth, dragging her deeper into his embrace. He groaned against her lips, and at the same time he rushed forward, seating himself fully inside her pussy.

Her eyes slid shut at the first thrust of his hard length inside her and she trembled in his arms, her pussy caving in around his cock. What the hell are you doing?

She asked herself for the thousandth time. This was crazy! She barely knew Mark, and yet she was letting him do things to her body that she'd never allowed any other man to do to her before.

She was always so responsible, but this was undoubtedly the craziest thing she'd ever done in her life. The worst part was that she loved every minute.

"God, Betty, you feel so good holding my cock," he moaned against her lips as he began to rock in and out of her on shallow strokes.

She tightened her thighs around him, as she let her hands roam across the muscled planes of his torso, still covered in his dress shirt.

She ached to rip it from him so that her bare hands could stroke his molded flesh, but that would only break his rhythm, which was quickly propelling her toward orgasm.

Her eyes flew open when he slammed into her, driving into her harder. She stared into his intense eyes, as sweat beaded along his hairline, and his face twisted from the effort of holding back his climax.

She rocked her hips off the desk, thrusting them forward to send him tunneling deeper inside her.

"Betty," he hissed.

"That's it Mark. Lose control of me. Come inside me," she rasped as her body began to tingle as the first wave of her climax grew inside her.

Throwing her head back, she caught his arms and screamed out his name at the same time he buried his length deep inside her and exploded, rushing his warm semen deep within her cover, drenching the spasming walls of her cunt.

Their cries of ecstasy mingled together, along with the essence of their orgasms, until they were both unable to form a word.

It was a long while before either of them moved, and when Mark did, she whimpered softly at the cold chill that settled over her with the loss of his warmth.

"It's alright, baby," he said, with a quick peck to her lips as he tucked himself back into his pants and straightened his clothing. "I'm just going to head to the bathroom to get us some paper towels."

"Ok," she mumbled, surprised she could even form a word. When the door closed behind him, she managed to find the strength to hop down from his desk, but her wobbly legs didn't seem to want to cooperate and she grasped the edge of his desk, sending papers and objects flying as she struggled to gain her footing.

"You're too old to be fucking on a desk," she said, with a low chuckle as she righted herself. When she felt steady on her feet, she stooped down to the floor to retrieve the objects she'd sent careening down there.

Most of the objects she'd scattered were papers, but she'd also toppled a few CDs. Clutching them in her hand, she shuffled through them to make sure she hadn't broken one.

She was almost done when her gaze landed on one CD that made everything inside her turn cold.

"Betty's Smith Account," she read the words scribbled across the disc in Mark's bold handwriting.

She sat down in his chair and popped the CD into the computer, but before the spreadsheets could even come up, she already knew what she would find there.

As she clicked through the files, she saw every single folder from the account she'd spent three months working on.

Anger the likes of which she'd never experienced bubbled up inside her. She could almost hear her heart shattering into tiny pieces at the thought that he'd lied to her just so that he could get into her pants while they worked long hours on an account that was already done, and like a fool, she'd fallen for his charming words.

"You're an idiot," she muttered, shaking her head.

The sound of the door opening drew her gaze, and as soon as he stepped inside, she pinned Mark with a hard glare as she stood to her feet.

He glanced between her and the computer screen, before returning his gaze to her, his eyes filled with remorse. He had better have felt some remorse, because he certainly had a lot to be remorseful for.

"I was going to tell you."

"When? After you got your fill of me and cast me aside."

His eyes widened as he crossed the room to stand before her, setting the paper towels he'd brought from the bathroom aside. He reached for her, but she protected away, the thought of him touching her was so upsetting that it nearly made her sick.

"That's not what this was about at all. I wasn't using you, Betty."

She stared at him in disbelief. "You lied to me Mark, so that you could use the time we spent together to seduce me."

"I did," he said taking a half step closer to her, forcing her back against his desk.

"I won't lie about that. It was wrong, I know this, and I'm sorry for lying to you. You were leaving and I didn't know how to keep you in my life, so I did something desperate."

"Desperate? This was beyond desperate. If you wanted me in your life, why didn't you simply ask me out like a normal person?"

Something about her words seemed to set him off, because storm clouds gathered in his blue eyes, and he grabbed her by her arms to drag her closer to him.

"I did ask you out. Several times, and several different ways, but you always just brushed me off.

For two years, I did this. I even bought you gifts for Christmas and your birthday. Last year I even bought you a Valentine's Day gift.

Most people would see those gestures as interesting, but not you. You thanked me politely, but then you did what you always do. You ignored me."

He let go of one arm to shove his hand through the tousled locks of his dark hair, as he released a long, ragged sigh.

"I apologized for my actions, they were wrong and deceitful, but you can't blame a guy for being desperate with you. It's been virtually impossible to get past the wall you put up."

She stared up at him, openmouthed, as small incidents from the past two years flashed through her head. She'd always thought he was just being polite, sucking up even. She'd never considered a man like him would even be remotely interested in her, so she'd ignored his subtle flirting and veiled compliments.

"Mark"

"You're sorry? I know that's what you were about to say, and you should be," he said, as he dragged her into his arms. "For two years I spent my time nursing this insane crush. But it's not a crush," he whispered, tunneling his hand into her hair, sending her hairpins crashing to the floor.

"After last night, I realized that there was something between us. She held his gaze, as countless emotions crossed his face, and she knew she probably wore the same expression.

Was it possible to fall for someone you barely knew? If it was, then she and Mark were certainly doing it.

"Mark, we're moving so fast. I want us to get to know each other better." Had she said that? Was she seriously considering dating him?

He tightened his arms around her, holding her closer, his face lighting up as he beamed down at her.

"That's all I ever wanted. A chance to get to know you. I won't lie and say that I'll take it much slower, because to be honest I know I'm already half in love with you."

He grinned when she gasped in shock, her eyes wide. She was still spinning from his revelation, but he didn't miss a beat.

"I want to give you time to fall for me too. I already know what I want, but when you commit to me, I want you to feel as certain of your decision, as I am of mine."

She arched a single brow. "Commitment? You're so sure of yourself now, aren't you?" She said, her lips curling into a teasing smile.

"I knew from the moment I met you that we would end up here. I didn't know how, but I was determined. Now it's time for you to realize what I've known all along."

"Really? And what's that?"

"That despite our differences and all the obstacles we have before us, there couldn't be two people in the world more perfect for each other."

CHAPTER 7

The Promise

Betty turned at the sound of the front door closing. Removing her glasses, she massaged the bridge of her nose and swiveled her chair around just in time to see Mark stroll into their home office dressed in a coal black business suit that fit his muscled frame perfectly.

She glanced at the clock above his head with a smile on her face. Six o'clock on the dot.

When they moved in together, he promised her he wouldn't turn into a workaholic just because of his new position, and thus far he'd kept his promise. But she knew he would.

Mark was a man of his word. She knew instinctively he'd quit before he broke his vow to her.

"How's my baby," he said with a smile as he kissed her soundly on the lips, taking his sweet time rediscovering the unique taste of her mouth.

She smiled when he lifted his head, before she glanced down to stroke her hand across her ever-expanding waist.

"He or she is fine."

He curled his lips into a grin. "I was talking about you. But how is my other baby too?"

He asked as he lovingly stroked his palm across her belly before he leaned down to kiss her stomach.

Dropping down into the chair across from her, he pulled it up, and tugged her feet into his lap to massage one swollen foot between his hands.

She laughed. "Both of us are fine. How was work?"

She forced herself not to giggle when he wrinkled his face up into a frown.

"Why didn't you tell me Jean was such an idiot? The marketing department is falling apart without you. You must come back," he complained.

"You've been saying that every day for the last eight months and every time you ask, I tell you no. I never thought I would like it so much, but I really enjoy consulting for retail companies and with the baby coming in a month the flexible schedule is ideal."

She leaned forward to place a quick peck against his lips when he continued to frown. "You guys will be fine without me."

She laughed when he shot her a pleading look. "That sad face will not work on me, and you know it, besides, you have nothing to be sad about.

You're doing an incredible job at Stone and tomorrow's your birthday."

A smile spread across his face as he leaned back into his chair.

"Ahh, I almost forgot about my birthday. Have you thought about the present I asked for?"

She had.

When they discovered she was pregnant, she'd agreed to move in with him. Not as slow as she wanted to take things, but it was as close as they could come to a compromise.

With a baby on the way, he'd wanted marriage, but she didn't, especially if it turned out they weren't compatible after all. She knew rushing into an ill-fated marriage would only make things worse in the end. But the reservations she had eight months ago were slowly starting to disappear.

Of the two of them, she truly questioned who was the wiser, because Mark seemed to know all along that they were good for each other, and he was right. She on the other hand had been cautious, wanting to take her time to be sure about them.

But with his birthday a day away, and the question he'd asked her months ago still pending over them, she'd come to realize that she'd never been surer of anything in her entire life.

She loved Mark and if he wanted them to be married before their child was born, then she would give him that.

"Well? What about my present?" he asked softly. She saw the doubts swirling in his eyes and she hated that he even doubted her, but she couldn't blame him.

Almost from day one, Mark had proclaimed his love for her over and over, but as usual, she'd taken just a bit longer to do the same.

The look on his face was like a fist closing around her heart. She never wanted him to question the depth of her feelings for him.

She leaned in again to caress his cheek with her palm. "I love you, honey."

His sapphire eyes sparkled when she said that. It had taken her so long to say the words, that she knew he treasured hearing them each time she said them. "I love you too," he said with a warm smile.

"So?" He surrounded her when she didn't finish, his expression anxious.

"So what? Tomorrow's your birthday, so you'll just have to wait until then to get your present," she said with a secret smile. "But I can promise you, you're going to love it."

"Betty," he groaned, but the joy on his face was unmistakable. Her heart flip flopped in her chest at the love she saw shining in his gaze.

His happiness was infectious, and she beamed at him as she leaned in closer to capture his lips in a searing kiss. Their lips melded so perfectly together, that she couldn't help but recall the words he'd said to her a long time ago.

There weren't two people in the world more perfect for each other than they were. She couldn't agree more.

THE END

THE CLASS REUNION

OVERVIEW

The Reunion tells the story of Diana Lopez, a talented opera singer who returns to her fifteen-year high school reunion to face her past. Her tarnished reputation and the man she left behind, Roberto Cruz.

Roberto never forgot Diana, but he questions whether love can survive fifteen years of separation until he comes face to face with her again.

He knows what he wants, and that is her. Now he must convince Diana to finally let go of her past to embrace the love that awaits them just on the horizon of the future.

CHAPTER 1

A Friendly Greeting

"Your name?"

The woman's eyes remained held on the paper in front of her face, forcing Diana to stare at the crown of her blonde head. Yet, despite the cloud of hair that obscured her face, Diana easily recognized the unmistakable delicate features of the woman, Rosa Lebron.

Diana blew out a long trembling breath, trying to decide if she should just run right then. No one had seen her yet and she was sure she could escape hidden if she got out of there right now, but before she could make a move, the woman lifted her head and she found herself staring into the enormous green eyes of the seemingly ageless woman.

Diana instantly glimpsed the awareness on her beautiful face.

At first, there was a flash of shock, followed by a moment of caution, until finally a peaceful politeness settled in her gaze.

She forced out a tight smile, thinking that it could have been worse.

Rosa could have blurted out her shock that the town whore had decided to show her face as she'd done all those years ago in high school.

Ahhh, but don't rule it out Diana. The night is still young.

"Diana." She cleared her throat. "Diana Sanchez."

"Hi, Diana. Welcome to the Bayside High Class of 93' Fifteen Year Reunion," Rosa said warmly as she stuck out a small rectangular object with her name emblazoned on it in bold black letters.

With shaky hands, she grasped the plastic nametag and pinned in on her chest.

"Thank you, Rosa," she said softly, acknowledging the woman by name. No sense in pretending they didn't know each other.

If she'd intended to do that then she could have just stayed at home. No sooner had the greeting escaped her lips, she was surprised to see a wide smile of genuine warmth spread across Rosa's face.

"You're welcome, Diana. I'm glad you came this year."

She nodded stiffly, as her eyes roamed over the lovely blonde's face, searching for any hint of carefully veiled scorn, but there appeared to be none.

Of all people, she'd expected Rosa to harbor the most resentment toward her. Hell, she would have resented her too. She'd slept with probably every single last one of Rosa's boyfriends while they were in high school. But strangely enough, Rosa seemed genuinely pleased that she'd decided to come. That shocked her.

She hadn't expected anyone to be kind to her, so she was taken aback by the woman's friendly greeting. Not knowing what else to say, she said nothing.

Instead, she dipped her head in a polite nod and turned away from her to walk toward the large gymnasium, a stiff smile plastered across her face.

Again, she considered tucking her tail and running like the yellow belly coward she was. This was a huge mistake. She should never have listened to her best friend Carmen.

So, Carmen was a world-renowned behavioral psychologist, she clearly didn't know what the hell she was talking about.

Diana was sure she didn't need to return to her high school to put her past to rest. She'd sworn to her friend that she'd dealt with her demons when her mother died, but Carmen had been stubborn.

"You missed your last two reunions. You must go to this one."

"Why?" Diana had protested as she frowned down into her friend's pretty, cocoa face. "I have no desire to be reminded of my high school years."

"But that's exactly what you need. You need to face the fact that you aren't that wounded young girl anymore," she argued.

"Once you do that then you will finally be able to move forward and have healthy relationships with men."

She wrinkled her nose. "I have healthy relationships with men."

Carmen snorted as she flung her long braids over her shoulder.

"If you mean boring, practically sexless relationships that are little more than platonic friendships."

"Sex complicates things."

"But it doesn't have to. Your relationships with boys in high school have prevented you from having fulfilling relationships with men as an adult."

Diana let out a weary sigh. "So, you think if I face all the boys I slept with in high school, that I'll what? Be able to put that part of my life into context?"

"I don't just think. I know. Once you face the fact that those guys and your experiences in high school do not define the person that you are today then I hope you will be able to realize that sex isn't something to be ashamed of in a relationship," she said quietly.

Diana had not missed the sympathetic look in Carmen's brown eyes or the sadness in her voice. She felt sorry for her. Hell, she felt sorry for herself too.

Despite years of therapy, she was still screwed up. Okay, maybe that wasn't entirely true, but at the very least she knew she still had issues concerning sex, men, and relationships.

A lot of it was due to her mother, but a lot of it also stemmed from her interactions with the opposite sex while in high school, and unfortunately, her experiences as a teen had left a lasting impression on her.

In a nutshell, she had once been the town tramp, and she hadn't quite been able to shake the label in her head, even after all these years.

The painful memories instantly flooded her causing her to weaken as the heel of her shoe caught a rung in the carpet, and she stumbled a few steps before catching herself.

She dragged in a deep breath and steadied herself. You are not that person anymore.

"You are a successful composer and mezzo soprano who has performed on stages across the world. You are sophisticated, beautiful, and brilliant.

This is not high school, and you are not that girl anymore," she said in a low voice, repeatedly. She chanted the same thing in her head with each step she took.

Running her hands down her stylish, but demure black cashmere dress, she took one last deep fortifying breath before she stepped inside the bustling gymnasium where the school colors of blue and gold hung from the ceiling as streamers, while balloons bounced back and forth against the strings where they were tied on all the chairs.

The party was in full swing, and music blasted loudly from the speakers, but as soon as she stepped inside, an almost welcome silence descended on the room.

Her heart tumbled and she froze like a deer caught in the headlights as all eyes shifted in her direction.

It was too late to run now. Everyone had seen her, and she knew what they all had to be thinking. The town slut was back.

CHAPTER 2

Roberto Cruz

The hair on the back of Roberto Cruz's neck stood for attention as an arc of lightning shot down his spine. He stiffened at the same time shocked gasps and a noise of low murmurs exploded like wildfire in the huge gymnasium.

He turned his attention away from Josefina Hernandez, one of the cheerleaders he'd known while he was the quarterback of Bayside's football team, and scanned the room, searching for the source of all the commotion, although something in his gut told him what, or rather who was now at the center of everyone's attention.

He'd always gotten a familiar tingling down his spine when she was close. He stepped closer toward the entrance of the gym at the same time his eyes landed on her.

He wanted her to look at him and as if she'd heard his thoughts, she turned her gaze toward him. A heavy knot tightened in his belly as soon as her beautiful cat-like hazel eyes met his.

He'd seen her performances on television and her picture in dozens of newspapers and magazines, but they still did not prepare him for the attack of emotions that flooded him at the first glimpse of the stunning brunette that had haunted almost all his high school fantasies, and many of his adult ones.

As if in a trance, he took a step toward her, but quickly came to his senses and stopped, wondering what the hell he was doing. She looked nervous and scared, and he wanted to go to her rescue and protect her as he'd done all those years ago, but he had no clue how she would receive him.

A dry smile lifted the corners of his lips. Probably in the same manner she'd received him the last time he'd tried to save her with great despise.

Back then, Diana hadn't been very trusting of people, him included, and he wondered if that had changed.

As he stared at her, he knew instinctively that he was willing to risk her disapproval

She just looked so afraid. Batting aside his reservations, he made his way toward her, but stopped again when Mario Forrest, the class DJ, stepped up to the microphone.

"If it isn't our very own, world celebrity opera singer, Diana Sanchez. Here's a shout out to Diana. I would play one of your CDs, but it's kind of hard to groove to if you know what I mean," he joked as he winked at her.

The entire room burst into laughter, while many applauded, and a few 'Way to go, Diana" cheers rang out over the music.

Roberto's eyes never left her face.

He could see that she was shocked, but he didn't miss the look of relief that flashed in her gaze. He visibly relaxed when most of the people turned their attention away from her and the tension in the air quickly began to dissolve.

A few of her former classmates now crowded around her, under the pretense of congratulating her. He snorted. More like just plain old sucking up.

Fifteen years ago, none of them would have come within ten feet of her, that is, unless you were a horny guy, and even then, when daylight came, none of them would have been caught dead with her.

He tightened his hands into fists as he struggled to temper the fury that always arose inside him every time, he thought of how Diana had suffered in high school. He'd hated how his entire class had treated her.

Not realizing that beneath the suggestive come ons, was a wounded and insecure girl, the guys had used her, and the girls who'd all been jealous of her obvious beauty and sensual charm, had thrown hurtful insults at her every chance they got.

Roberto chuckled dryly to himself as he watched the phony spectacle unfold right there before his eyes as more and more people pleaded around her to get her autograph.

Served them all right to now must crawl at her feet. She had always been truly gifted and talented, but no one had taken the time to look deeper except you, a tiny voice shouted in his head, but he shook it away. Yeah, but it didn't mean a damn thing. He thought bitterly.

At the end, she still hadn't cared that he saw beneath the front she showed the world.

At the end, she'd put him in the same category as all the other guys and he'd let her.

Fifteen Years Ago....

Roberto had been raised in a home full of Rachmaninoff, Chopin, and Schubert so he knew Beethoven's famous Moonlight Sonata when he heard it, but the roaming lilt of the light voice that accompanied it sent chills down his spine.

Football practice had just ended, so he'd been on his way to his locker to pick up his history book, before he headed home.

But at the sound of the riveting music, he stopped in his tracks and walked in the opposite direction, down the hallway toward the music room.

He wrinkled his brow into a frown as he drew closer to the room. It was almost six o'clock, much too late for a young woman to be alone in the deserted school. He rounded the corner and leaned against the open doorway, expecting to find a naïve freshman sitting at the piano.

Who else would sneak into the school with no regard for her safety? But as soon as his gaze settled on the figure behind the piano, he quickly realized that he was completely and utterly wrong. He nearly collapsed to his feet when he saw who it was.

Diana?

He shook his head and refocused his gaze. He'd always suspected that behind her frightened eyes, waited a troubled young woman, who possessed great emotional depth, despite the shallow front she presented.

But still, he'd had no idea that the same troubled girl was so amazingly talented. He stared in amazement, listening to her hot voice as it climbed to the soprano range and hovered there.

She had a beautiful voice and it calmed him into a trance, wrapping around him like a warm blanket.

He stood there gazing at her in silence, appreciating the rare treat of seeing her stripped bare in her true element. The young woman before him was the real Diana, the one who poured her heart into a timeless song, and he was humbled by this intimate glimpse inside her soul.

He let his gaze slide over her, drinking in her exquisite features, as she played the final notes to the song. Her inky black hair hung to her waist in soft waves completely unbound, framing her lovely face like a halo.

He sat behind her in biology class and many times he'd ached to reach out and slide his fingers through her silky curls.

He continued his gentle exploration of her figure. Though he couldn't see much of her with the piano obstructing his view, he knew from memory that she was blessed with generous curves along her flexible frame.

In every way, she was a natural beauty, so beautiful, that in his mind, she didn't have to sleep around to get any man's attention. She already had it. From the moment she walked into a room, she had everyone's attention including his, especially his.

The music stopped and without thinking he lifted his hands and clapped. She gasped softly, her eyes growing wide as saucers as her creamy cheeks turned pink with embarrassment.

He stepped inside the room, folded his arms across his chest and supported one hip against the piano.

"That was beautiful."

"Thank you," she said softly as she dipped her gaze toward the piano keys, the blush growing darker by the moment. He grinned, thinking that she looked adorable when she was embarrassed.

"Who taught you how to play, to sing?"

She shrugged as she stood up from the bench. "No one. I just listened to cassettes of Mozart, Beethoven, Jessye Norman, and a whole bunch of other folks that I got from the library..." her voice trailed off and she shrugged again.

"And then I just mimicked what I heard."

He stared at her open mouthed. Her talent could rival some of the best opera singers in all of Europe, and she'd taught herself! He was speechless.

"I can't believe you learned how to play from just listening to the music. Even your voice sounds as if you've had training.

Diana, that's amazing." He knew he was flowing, but he couldn't help it. He had an admiration for Diana.

She immersed her head and stepped around him. "Whatever," she said jokily, brushing off the compliment.

She stooped down to grab her book bag. But when she stood back up, all traces of the shy and embarrassed girl were gone and in her place was the airless vixen he was used to seeing.

She stepped closer, her full breasts brushing against his chest, forcing him to bite back a low groan as he swallowed hard, but he didn't move.

You don't have to lie to me, Roberto, to get what you really want," she whispered seductively, her lips just inches from his ear, as her warm breath feathered across his sensitive skin.

Despite his best effort not to, he could not stop the tremor of desire that raced through him.

Yet, despite the fog of lust that had suddenly wrapped around him, those simple words were like a bucket of ice being thrown over his head.

He grasped her by the shoulders and held her away from him.

"Why do you do that?"

She stared at him in shock. She probably was in shock. Probably the first time a man had ever turned down the invitation she'd so obviously extended to him.

"You're beautiful and talented. So beautiful that you don't have to do the things you do to get a man to like you and too talented not to realize that there is more to you than just your beauty."

She rolled her eyes and turned her head to stare out the window, her jaw set in defiance.

He released one shoulder and cupped her chin in his hand, tilting her head toward him to force her gaze back to his face. The tears that shimmered in her eyes tore at his heart, but he was happy to see them.

They proved that Diana wasn't as unaffected as she pretended to be. He knew there was more to her than the femme act she liked to put on.

For some reason, she hid that person, preferring instead to live in the shadow of the vixen she presented to the world.

He held her gaze, wanting to say more to convince her that he wasn't just feeding her lines of bullshit, but he made the mistake of letting his gaze drifted to her full, pouty lips.

He groaned aloud. Many times, he'd stared at her lips wondering if they tasted as ripe as they looked. He ached to kiss her as his eyes remained fixed on her tempting mouth.

Her lips were just so lush and succulent as if begging for his kiss, and before he realized what was happening, he found himself lowering his head slowly, to capture her mouth with his.

Her eyes drifted shut and she tilted her head further back to press her lips fully against his. He closed his own eyes and just let himself feel.

Running his tongue back and forth against her lips, he teased her luscious flesh until she opened her mouth and let him in. She moaned into his mouth as he swept inside the moist cavern and tasted her. She reminded him of sweet fruit, sweet, honeyed nectar.

He snaked his arms around her waist and dragged her flush against his hard body. He didn't even try to hide the evidence of his arousal as he rocked his hard erection against her belly.

She lifted her arms to twine them behind his neck, and her full breasts flattened against his muscular torso, her large nipples stabbing him through the rough fabric of their clothing.

He held her tightly against him, savoring her sweet warmth as he plundered her lush mouth for several long minutes, drawing throaty moans from her until he could feel her body beginning to quiver. But when she slid a single hand down to cup his hardening length, he instantly froze.

This was headed exactly where he didn't want it to go. With great reluctance, he pulled away from her, disentangling his body from her arms.

She stared up at him, her face flushed red, and her eyes wide.

"Why did you stop?" The words came out as a husky protest, and he struggled not to let them affect him, even as his cock tightened against the zipper of his jeans, begging him to release it from its confines to settle inside the wet warmth of the woman who was responsible for his current state.

But he didn't take her back into his arms. He refused to finish what he'd started.

"Because I want you to know that there is at least one guy at Bayside who wants more from you than what you offer."

That wasn't entirely true. He wanted what she offered too, but he also wanted more. She narrowed her eyes at him. "Don't act like you're so polite, Roberto.

At the end men all want the same thing, one thing."

"I won't lie to you and say that I don't want that too. You're beautiful and you know it, and yes, I want you, but that's not all I want."

She cocked her head to the side, her eyes flashing with suspicion.

"Then what is it that you do want?"

He bent down to scoop her backpack in his hand, which she'd dropped during their kiss and slung it over his shoulder. "I want to get to know the real you, the real Diana."

"Why?" She said with narrowed eyes.

Why? Because he'd had a crush on her ever since freshman year, but never acted on it because the thought of becoming another notch on her bedpost didn't sit well with him.

That's what he thought, but of course he didn't tell her any of that.

Instead, he shrugged and said, "Because I think I would like the real Diana better than the one I know now."

He turned away from her and strolled toward the door, leaving her standing there, as he ignored her still skeptical expression. He couldn't fault her for being mistrustful of his intentions.

There were probably a few guys who wanted to take the time to get to know the real Diana. But he was one of them.

"Come on. I'll drive you home."

"I don't need you to drive me home. Besides, practice just ended and someone may see you with me."

His hand tightened around the strap of her book bag as he stared down at her, recognizing the insult for what it was, even if she didn't realize she'd just insulted him.

Because of her reputation, most guys shunned Diana, that is when they weren't trying to sleep with her. Cruel as it seemed, she was probably used to it, came to expect it even, but he was insulted that she thought he was that big of an asshole. He'd been raised better than that.

It was late and dark, and he wasn't going to allow her to walk home alone.

"I don't care who sees us. Now come on. I'm taking you home."

He spun away from her and stomped out of the room then, not even bothering to look back to make sure she followed. He was too angry to look back anyway.

As his grandmother always said, only fools and cowards died under the weight of gossip and rumors, and he would like to think he was neither. He didn't care who saw them.

CHAPTER 3

The Punch

Diana tipped her head back and downed her third glass of punch in a single gulp, wishing she had something stronger.

She was trying to work up the nerve to march over to Roberto and say hello, but she was finding it harder than she'd imagined it would be. She'd been following him with her eyes pretty much since she walked into the room, but he was never alone, and what she had to tell him was for his ears only.

Carmen may have thought she needed to come back to her reunion to lay her past to rest, but Diana knew the real reason she was there.

She'd been in school and couldn't afford to take the trip for her fifth year reunion, and then she'd been in Europe on tour for the tenth, but the current tour she was on was in the United States, so she saw her fifteenth-year reunion as the perfect opportunity.

This is the perfect opportunity to see Roberto and thank him.

"Stop lying to yourself, girl. You want to do more than just thank him," she muttered under her breath. Okay, she could admit it; she still held a heavy crush on the handsome, unattainable star quarterback of the football team. Even before he'd shown any genuine interest in her, she, like all the other girls in school, had salivated over the blonde hunk.

In high school she'd tried a couple of times to flirt with him, but he always seemed disinterested, bored even. Back then his actions had really

75

stung her pride. There wasn't a boy at Bayside that she couldn't bed, except Roberto Cruz.

Roberto was the only one who turned her down more times than she could count. Even after they'd become sort of friends, things had never gone very far.

At the time it had been frustrating. His cold shoulder toward her had nagged at her and with her self-esteem as low as it had been back then, she'd take on his rejection.

Back then, she convinced herself that Roberto didn't want her because he thought he was too good for her. She couldn't blame him.

In her mind, he was. It wasn't until she became an adult that she realized Roberto had been a man who lived up to his word. He'd been trying to show her that her true worth didn't come from lying on her back, and he'd been serious about keeping his hands off her to prove it.

Roberto's actions toward her had helped her realize her sense of self-worth and eventually led to a turning point in her life. She knew she owed a great deal of her success to him and his belief in her.

Now, she wanted him to know that. She gulped down another glass of punch, knowing she was going to have to pee soon if she kept this up. She chucked the empty plastic cup in the waste basket nearby as she dragged in a deep breath and gathered up her courage.

She was just about to go in search of Roberto when a deep familiar voice washed over her like a gentle breeze.

"I can tell you that if you're looking to get drunk, you should probably try something far stronger than Hawaiian Punch."

She turned around, her eyes wide in surprise. Her eyes grew bigger when she realized Roberto only stood about two feet away from her, much closer than she'd expected.

"Roberto. Hi," she squeaked. Her stomach flip flopped, and she wanted to hang her head and wait for the earth to just open and swallow her. She was so embarrassed. She sounded like Minnie Mouse on speed.

He stepped closer to her, edging into her personal space, causing her heart to beat faster. She felt trapped and suffocating, all at the same time, but she didn't move. She simply lifted her chin to meet his gaze, holding her ground.

"Were you ever planning to come say hello or were you just going to stare at me all night?"

She blinked furiously as heat rushed to her cheeks. She cleared her throat trying to stop her silly babbling.

"You were never alone. I wanted to talk to you alone."

He smiled that heart stopping smile where his dimples in both cheeks popped out and his eyes twinkled. She resisted the urge to fan herself, but damn it was getting hot in there.

"That's funny. Because I wanted to talk to you alone too. Do you have time to have dinner with me?"

She gazed. "Tonight?"

He shrugged. "I'll be here for the week visiting my parents, so it doesn't have to be tonight. But the night is young, and this finger food has only served to make me angry so I was hoping you would join me."

She smiled at his words because she knew he was telling the truth.

Chicken tenders and a veggie plate would make her angry too if she were 6'6

and 270 pounds of solid muscle.

She was surprised he hadn't already passed out from hunger pangs.

"Well, I'm still on tour right now and I'll only be here for two more days so I guess it will have to be dinner tonight or not at all."

His face lit up at her words and he held out his elbow. "Great. Then shall we go?"

She nodded as she tucked her arm in his and allowed him to usher her out of the school, all the while pretending she didn't see the shocked expressions of her classmates as they walked by.

Inwardly, she rolled her eyes knowing without a doubt that the gossip line in the small town of Bayside Florida would be on fire all night long regaling the tale of the wicked extravagant daughter's return to Bayside to tangle the town's most upstanding son.

Ahhh, but some things never changed.

CHAPTER 4

Unwanted Welcome

Diana pulled her rented Ford Focus into the parking space beside Roberto's car and cut the engine. Grabbing her purse, she took his outstretched hand as he helped her out of her car, and with their hands still clasped together, they walked toward the front door.

The drive there had been pretty much a blur, so she got her first glimpse of the restaurant as she neared the entrance, and as soon as she did, her steps hesitated.

She thought she'd recovered rather quickly, but her hesitation must have shown on her face, because Roberto turned to her and asked, "Is there something wrong?"

She flashed him a small smile. "I guess I was expecting someplace a little more….casual," she said as she glanced up at the sign for Alain Ducasse, the ultra-chic, upscale French restaurant just outside Bayside in the small, but popular town of Summerville.

Roberto eyes twinkled as he smiled. "You're an international superstar. I couldn't just take you to a burger Place."

She grinned at the teasing gleam in his eyes. "Yes, you could have, and I would have been just fine."

"But I wouldn't have," she said, scrunching his face into a frown.

"I think I overdosed on burgers as a kid. The thought of another Triple M Deluxe Burger makes me want to puke."

She chuckled at the sour expression on his face. "Alright, then French it is," she said as she let him escort her inside.

In moments, they were seated at a secluded table tucked away in a corner that allowed them a great deal of privacy. Diana was grateful.

Her face wasn't so noticeable that she got stalked like a Halle Berry or Angelina Jolie, but she was still known by many and sometimes she found private moments could quickly turn into awkward public spectacles, which was the last thing she wanted to happen tonight.

She just wanted to enjoy a quiet dinner with an old friend in peace and complete privacy.

"I was surprised that you came back this year. When I saw your name on the list, I thought someone had made a mistake."

A tiny grin tugged at her lips as she shifted her gaze from unfolding her linen napkin in her lap to Roberto's face.

"I think everyone was surprised, including me."

He cocked his head to the side and studied her with curious eyes, causing her to fidget in her chair under the weight of his scrutiny. "Why'd you come back?"

The question was innocent enough, but there was a wealth of meaning behind it and they both knew it.

"For many reasons." Heat crept into her cheeks, and she looked away feeling slightly embarrassed.

"The main one being that I needed to prove to myself that I was over my past."

"And are you?"

She dragged her eyes back to his face, and just drowned in the crystal clear blue depths of his eyes.

"I'm as over it as I'll ever be," she said truthfully, knowing that one could never truly escape their past, but they could at the least come to terms with it, which is what she had done by coming back.

"And the other reason? For coming back," He added when she shot him a puzzled look. She smiled at him.

"To see you."

"Me?"

"Yes, you. I wanted to say thank you."

"'Thank you' for what?"

She held his gaze. "For changing my life. I know it sounds silly and a little cliché, but I never forgot how you treated me the last semester of our senior year.

The things you said to me stayed with me and I owe a lot of my belief in myself at that time to you."

"Me?"

She chuckled softly at the comical look of shock plastered across his face.

She reached across the table and gripped his hand with her own.

"Yes, you, Roberto. I wanted to thank you in person," she said softly and released his hand abruptly when shocks of warmth skated from her fingertips all the way up her arm.

"I don't know what to say. I mean, I don't remember saying much.

I really can't take credit for the person you've become."

"And I'm not giving you credit for the person I've become," she joked, her eyes sparkling with laughter. "But I am giving you credit for helping me realize that I wanted to be more than what I was."

He smiled. "And here I thought I was going to get a finder's cut or something."

"I'm sorry to disappoint you there," she said, shaking her head as she chuckled as his words.

He let out a long-suffering sigh and she found herself laughing harder. "Well then, I guess I'll just have to settle for that heartfelt thank you." Laughter shimmered in his eyes for a few more moments before his expression turned serious.

"I still don't think I deserve any thanks but you're welcome, Diana. I'm proud of you and I was happy to hear of your successes over the years.

You deserve it."

She avoided her gaze under the weight of his stare, feeling just a little embarrassed by the look of pride in his eyes.

She would never admit it, but it warmed her inside to know that he was proud of the person she'd become. She still wasn't the same girl who desperately sought the approval of others, but she was happy to know that she had Roberto's.

"Ohmigod, I'm so stuffed. I forgot how rich French food is."

Roberto wagged his eyebrows at her from over the menu. "So, you're sure, you don't want dessert."

"Oh, don't tempt me. I would love to but I'm going to bust out of this dress if I eat another bite."

He grinned. "Alright then, but don't complain later that you wish you'd ordered the Crème Brule when I'm digging in."

"Oh, you're so evil," she said with a short pout.

She scowled at him for a few seconds before they both burst into fits of laughter at her antics.

As their laughter died down, they settled into a comfortable silence until their waiter returned. Despite his teasing, he declined dessert and quickly settled the bill.

"Thank you for dinner. It was great seeing you again and I had a wonderful time."

Roberto struggled to school his features into a pleasant mask as he tried to hide his disappointment.

He didn't want the night to end, but he couldn't think of an excuse to extend it.

He opened his mouth to ask her out to lunch tomorrow but never got the chance when unpleasant crows of laughter floated across the partition. He would have ignored it had he not recognized the familiar voices coming from just a few feet away.

"Did you see her? "Ohmigod. I can't believe she had the nerve to show up and then she comes back expecting everyone to fawn all over her like she is some big-time celebrity."

"Why do you think she came back after all this time?"

"I don't know. Probably to add Roberto to her list of conquests. Did you see the way she was draped all over him? What a whore. Still the same old Diana."

Roberto stiffened when Jessica and Steve, his old football buddy from school, broke out into another round of laughter.

His eyes snapped into Diana's face. She sat there stiff as a board, but if the words had had any effect on her, she didn't show it.

He immediately jumped to his feet, already headed toward the table on the other side of the wall where he was prepared to ruin Steve and Jessica's dinner just as they'd just ruined his, but he was forced to stop when Diana stood and blocked his way.

He grasped her arms and tried to physically put her back down into her seat, but she wouldn't budge.

He could have overpowered her, but he didn't when she silently mouthed the words. "Let's just go."

He shook his head vehemently, but eventually relented when he glimpsed the pleading look in her eyes.

He nodded reluctantly; his jaw set in a tight frown as he clasped her hand in his and stalked angrily out of the restaurant, trying to be mindful not to drag her behind him in his rush to get out of there before he ignored her request and went back inside to do what he longed to do.

He stormed outside to the parking lot, and with his free hand pressed the button on his key chain. The car alarm beeped and as soon as the locks popped up, he reached for the handle to open the passenger door.

"Roberto, I drove my car."

"I would like to go somewhere so that we can talk in private. I'll drive you back here."

"No, Roberto. Thank you for dinner, but I'm tired and I'm going back to the hotel."

He glimpsed the resolve in her eyes and before he could stop her, she wrenched her hand from his, hopped into her car and pealed out of the parking lot.

"Diana!" He slammed his palm against the hood of his car. "Damnit."

Not stopping to think about what he was doing, he jumped into his car, turned on the ignition and tore out of the parking lot after her.

CHAPTER 5

The Setup

Shit!" Diana cursed as she angrily swiped at the tears that slipped down her cheeks. She had fought hard to keep them from spilling in front of Roberto, so she was proud that she managed to hold it together long enough for her to make it into the safety of her car.

It had been so long since she'd let the cruel names get to her.

"You're becoming soft," she chuckled bitterly. Back in school she'd been prepared for them so she'd forged a wall of steel and kept her emotions locked up tight behind it.

But now, now she wasn't quite as prepared as she used to be. Still the words hurt just as bad now as they did then.

"What did you expect, you idiot. You knew what people were thinking," she argued with herself. Yes, it was bad enough knowing what people were thinking, but worse to hear it from their lips.

She glanced into her rearview mirror and swore again. Roberto was still following her. What the hell was he doing? She didn't want to talk to him. Not right now. She was too humiliated. It always seemed as if he was constantly present to witness some of her lowest moments.

"Apparently, it's becoming a habit." She swiped the last bit of moisture from her cheeks and pressed down on the accelerator, hoping he would take the hint and leave her alone.

She sped all the way back to the center of town until she pulled into the parking lot of the Bayside Marriot.

Jumping out of her car, she stalked angrily toward the silver BMW that pulled up beside her. He barely had a chance to cut the ignition before she was flinging open his door.

"What the hell is wrong with you?"

Much to her annoyance, he didn't miss a beat as he unfolded his large frame from his car and towered over her, his face twisted with fury.

"I could say the same thing to you. You broke every speed limit all the way back here."

"Because you were following me. It should have been obvious that I was trying to get away from you," she shouted, before she realized that the parking lot wasn't as empty as she'd thought it was when she saw curious onlookers stopping to stare at them.

"Come on before we cause a scene," she snapped under breath as she twisted around on her heels and stomped inside to the lobby, not once glancing back to see if he followed. She stabbed impatiently at the elevator button and waited until the metal doors finally parted.

Stepping inside, she pressed the button for her floor and leaned against the wall, silently fuming as she folded her arms across her chest.

She could feel the anger radiating from Roberto as he stood closer to her than she would have liked, but she ignored him. He had no right to be angry. He wasn't the one who'd been stalked all the way back to his hotel and forced into an embarrassing public confrontation.

When the elevator came to a stop on her floor, she pulled out her key card and walked in the direction of her room. Swiping the card into the lock, she twisted the handle and stepped inside.

As soon as the door slammed shut, she turned on Roberto, prepared to lay into him, but he beat her to it.

"Why didn't you stand up for yourself back there?"

"What?"

He took a step toward her, his face red with anger. "In high school you used to just let people insult you while you stood by and said nothing and tonight you did the same thing. You just took it."

"Roberto, when you're used to being insulted on a regular basis you learn how to deal with it the best way you can."

"Which is by rolling over and just taking it. By letting people get away with hurting you and not standing up for yourself."

Every muscle in Diana's body tensed at the disappointment she heard in his voice. He had no right to make her feel as if she lacked a backbone just because she chose to rise above the name calling. She narrowed her eyes as she clenched her hands into tight fists.

If Roberto thought she was a push over then he was sadly mistaken. Just because she chose her battles wisely and didn't mean she was some kind of coward.

"You are still the same self-righteous S.O.B that you always were. Don't talk to me about standing up for myself.

I may not choose to fight with ignorant and stupid people who insult me out of jealousy, but at least I had the guts to fulfill my dreams and not the dreams everyone else had for me. When it came to mapping out my future at least I had the courage to stand up for myself, unlike you."

The color drained from his face, and she knew she'd hit her mark when his lips tightened at the corners. She took a step forward, closing the distance between them.

"All your words were just a bunch of bullshit. In the end you let your parents dictate your life, and you became a surgeon just like your father and your brother. I guess fixing noses and doing tummy tucks could be considered a form of architecture."

"I suggest you stop while you're ahead since you don't know what the hell you're talking about."

"Oh, I know what I'm talking about. I know you still feel pressure to live up to your brother and your parents' expectations."

Her next words lodged in her throat when he suddenly seized her by the arms with both hands, his blue eyes darkening as storm clouds of anger swirled in their depths.

She opened her mouth to tell him to release her, but before she could even get that out, he lowered his head and crushed his lips against hers.

She was so shocked by the unexpected action that for several seconds she just stood there, stiff as a board, but when his tongue swept against the seam of her mouth, coaxing her to open for him, she melted against him.

He robbed her mouth with his hot, searing kiss as anger poured off his body like hot lava. Liquid heat pooled at her core, and she had to clamp her thighs together to keep the sticky wetness from dampening her thighs.

Sensing her capitulation, he shoved his hand into her hair, forcing her head back, as he deepened the kiss, his mouth hungrily devouring hers from the inside out.

Everything about him was hard and demanding as he ravished her with his lips until she completely yielded to him, her body collapsing into a boneless, trembling mess against the strength of his muscled frame.

Her nipples pebbled against his chest, and she moaned into his mouth at the feel of his cock hardening against her belly.

As if his own arousal triggered something inside him, he pulled his mouth from hers, his chest heaving as he stared down into her face.

Still gripping her hair with his fist, he lowered his forehead to rest against hers and closed his eyes, a weary sigh escaping him.

"Why do I always do this with you? After all these years, you would think I'd learn to control myself around you."

Lifting his head, he opened his eyes, although he kept his hand tangled in her hair. "I've always believed in you. Always thought the best of you, but you can never do the same for me."

His words tore at her like a sharp knife, and the mixture of regret and pain that flashed across his face, caused the knife to sink in deeper.

She opened her mouth to apologize, but never got the chance when he abruptly shoved her away from him and twisted on his heels to march across the room.

"Good night, Diana," he said quietly and then he closed the door behind him with a soft click, effectively shutting her out of his life for good.

A gasp tore past her lips when a hand clamped around her upper arm. She turned around, her heart slamming against her chest.

"Roberto? Good grief. You scared the shit out of me."

"Don't go in there, Diana."

She glanced at the door and then back at him. "Why not?"

"Kevin lied to you. It's not just him in there."

She wrinkled her brow, her lips dipping into a frown. "What are you are talking about?"

"Come with me and I'll show you."

"But Kevin is expecting me."

Impatience flashed across his face. "Diana, just trust me, alright?"

She rolled her eyes and sucked her teeth but finally nodded. "Fine."

She walked beside him until she realized they were headed to his car. She started to protest again, but snapped her mouth shut at the exasperated look on his face.

With a heavy sigh, she let him help her into the passenger seat and waited for him to show her whatever it was that he was so determined to show her.

They drove for about ten seconds until they pulled up to the side of Kevin's first story apartment. She'd known Kevin throughout high school, but she'd never given him the time of day.

He was handsome enough, but he'd always seemed a little weird to her, as if something was off about him. But then he graduated, and somehow, he seemed cooler, more sophisticated now that he was a freshman at Bayside Community College.

So, when she ran into him at a party a couple of nights ago, she'd let him have her number this time. She hadn't been surprised when he'd called her last night to invite her over to watch a movie.

He'd expressed his interest in her many times before. But what had surprised her was running into Roberto right outside Kevin's apartment.

She twisted her head around to glare at Brad. "Alright, what is it that you must show me?"

"Just look through the window."

She turned her head in the direction he pointed and focused her gaze on the window that allowed her to see into Kevin's apartment. The curtains were pulled back, so she was able to get a clear glimpse inside.

"What do you see?" Roberto whispered close to her ear. She gasped, and her bottom lip began to tremble when her eyes settled on the chilling scene before her.

She swallowed hard as she tried to keep the tears from slipping down her cheeks. About half of the football team, plus several guys she didn't know, all crowded inside the tiny apartment.

The guys stood around with bottles and cans of beer cupped in their hands, while music blared loudly all the way outside.

It looked like a party, except there were no girls. She whipped her head around to stare at Roberto.

"How did you know about this?"

A wary look crossed his face. "I was invited. I waited outside in my car until I saw you walk up; I knew what he had planned, and I just couldn't…."

He let out a weary sigh and turned away from her to start the car. "I'll take you home."

She reached out a hand to grip his forearm. "I don't want to go home right now. Can you take me back to school? Music helps me sort things out." She added when he shot her a puzzled look.

He simply nodded and they drove to school in silence. Her mind was a jumble of conflicting thoughts as she sat beside him.

She knew Kevin hadn't invited her over just for a movie, but the thought that he'd planned something so wicked was beyond her comprehension.

She gulped deeply trying to fight back the panic as she imagined what could have happened had Roberto not got involved.

Anger and helplessness raged inside her. Kevin thought with her reputation that she could be treated in such a manner and while it angered her, she almost couldn't blame him.

Nobody would have believed her and even if they did, they would have all argued that she deserved it. Every guy in that room would have gotten away with it and more labels would have been attached to her reputation.

She knew who she was and what she was, but that didn't mean she deserved what he had planned, nobody did.

Her mind was so far away from the present that it took her several seconds to realize that Roberto had parked the car and was already hopping out.

She cast a cautious glance up at him when he opened the passenger door and helped her out. She thought he would just drop her off but instead, he followed her inside and sat in one of the chairs, waiting in patient silence as she teased her fingers over the keys until she finally settled on Rachmaninoff's Isle of the Dead.

As her fingers skimmed over the ivory keys, she lost herself in the moment and completely forgot he was there as she let her voice join in the melody of the haunting music.

She played for what seemed like hours, although it couldn't have been more than fifteen minutes.

When she finally stopped, she felt as if she was coming out of a trance. It was always like that when she played. She would lose herself to the music, leaving everything else behind.

"I've never seen someone so passionate about something the way you are about your music."

A small smile lifted the corners of her lips as she stood from the bench and crossed the room to where Roberto now stood staring out the window.

"That can't be true. Everyone is passionate about something and I'm sure you've seen it in others besides me."

He shrugged. "I guess, but I've never seen someone follow their passion the way you do."

She snorted. "Don't give me too much credit. The only reason why I even applied to Barnard and the Peabody Conservatory is because you told Mrs. Owens and she pulled some strings to get me an audition."

"But you did it. You didn't hesitate. You sent in your application and went to the auditions. I admire that."

A tiny thrill of pleasure settled in her belly at the admiration she heard in his voice. But she quickly pushed it aside, not wanting to read more into it than there was.

Instead, she focused her attention solely on him. There was something about what he said and how he said it that gave her pause.

He sounded almost wistful, envious even. She stepped toward him, studying him closer.

"What's your passion, Roberto?"

He stared at her in shock, as if she'd read his mind. She would have laughed if she'd thought he wouldn't take offense. Anyone with two eyes and half a brain could guess what was on his mind.

He stood up straight, his eyes boring into her. "Promise me you won't laugh?"

"Why would I laugh?"

"And swear to me you won't tell anyone."

She wanted to remind him that she had no friends to tell, but instead, she said, "I swear."

"Alright, follow me."

She stared after him, her expression curious, before she took off behind him.

They navigated the deserted corridors of the school until they got to his locker. He fumbled with the code until it unlocked, and he pulled the door open.

She peaked inside and saw a couple of AC/DC bumper stickers and some books, but not much else. He stooped down on his upper leg and rummaged through the books until he pulled out a large pad.

She glanced down at the pad in his hands, and then up at his face, which was now tinged with red. She narrowed her eyes. He was nervous. But why?

"Can I take a look?" She finally asked when he just stood there in silence clutching the tablet. He nodded and slowly handed it over.

She flipped open the cover. She stood there in stunned silence as she carefully drummed through each page.

Most of the images were of landscapes and buildings, but there were a few sketches and drawings of people. Her eyes grew wide when her gaze landed on a picture of her own face.

"I can explain that."

"Ohmigod. Roberto, this is brilliant." She flipped through the rest of the pages until she came to an end.

"You're an artist. An amazing one.

Why doesn't anyone know about this?"

He shrugged; his expression sheepish.

"You know."

She frowned at him. "You know what I mean. In the yearbook it says you're going to school for pre-med but it's obvious you need to be somewhere studying art and architecture."

She stared at him in admiration.

"Roberto, this is your passion. Why are you not pursuing it?"

He twisted his lips into a frown and looked away from her. "My father is a surgeon. My brother just got accepted to med school."

He let out a long sigh and turned his head back around to face her. The look in his eyes made her heart sink. Before he even spoke, she knew what he was going to say, and it saddened her.

"I will disappoint everyone if I don't become a surgeon too."

"You convinced me to go to school for music and here you are bending to the will of your family. Don't you think that's awfully hypocritical of you?"

She instantly regretted her words when his expression hardened and he reached out to snatch the pad from her hands and tossed it back inside his locker, slamming the door shut with a loud bang.

He glared at her. "You don't know what it's like to have the weight of your family's expectations on your shoulders."

"You're right. I don't. But I know talent when I see it and I can tell you it would be a waste not to do anything with it."

She could tell he was furious when the muscle in his jaw twitched as he clenched his teeth together.

"It's getting late. I better take you home," he gritted out as he brushed past her.

"Yeah, whatever," she snapped back as she trailed after him, her eyes burning angry holes into his back.

CHAPTER 6

Diana's Confusion

For the second time in as many days Diana asked herself "What the hell am I doing here?"

It wasn't too late to run away this time. Nobody knew she was driving a blue Focus and if she could make it to her car before anyone answered the door, she could spare herself from making a dreadful mistake.

She turned around, all set to do an all-out hurry to the car when she heard the lock turn.

"Damnit," she cursed and turned around just as the door swung open to reveal a beautiful middle-aged woman with warm eyes the same delicate blue as Roberto's.

She cracked her lips into a tentative smile. "Hi. Um, my name Is…."

"Oh my. Oh my. Please come in. Oh my. This is quite a surprise,"

the woman babbled as she seized Diana's arm and practically dragged her inside.

The woman fanned herself as if she was having a hot flash. "I cannot believe the Diana Sanchez is in my home.

Martha is going to have a fit when I tell her. Come in, dear. Do you want anything, tea, coffee, Diana's mouth felt open as she allowed herself to be dragged along behind Roberto's mother into the kitchen. She hadn't really thought of the reception she would receive, but she certainly hadn't been expecting this.

Diana found herself being dropped down into a chair as the woman fussed for about thirty seconds on what to serve her.

When she finally paused to take a breath, Diana cut in.

"Mrs. Cruz, that is very kind of you. But I don't want anything to eat or drink. I'm just here to speak to Roberto."

The woman smiled warmly as she smacked the heel of her hand against her forehead. "Oh yes, of course. The reunion. I forgot you and Roberto were in the same class."

She sucked her teeth and pouted, and Diana fought hard not to laugh. "And here I thought Oprah was granting me a wish or something."

This time Diana did laugh as she instantly relaxed in the presence of the charming woman. She shook her head then.

"I'm sorry to disappoint you, Mrs. Cruz. But, nope, no Oprah, just me," she smiled as she lifted her shoulders.

The woman chuckled, waving her hand in the air. "Please, call me Barbara. And are you sure I can't get you anything? The boys went off to play a round of golf with their father this morning.

They should be home any minute. You are welcome to stay and have lunch with us."

Barbara seemed earnest enough, but she shook her head. Roberto would not appreciate being forced to share a meal with her, especially after last night.

"Again, thank you, but I can't stay. I just wanted to speak with Roberto before I left." She stood at her feet. "Can you please tell him I said good-bye?"

"You can tell me yourself."

Diana turned around at the sound of the deep, husky voice that sent chills down her spine. Her stomach fell to her feet when her eyes clashed with his. There was a wealth of emotion in his gaze.

Most of it was anger, but there was also something else there too. Goosebumps broke out across her skin as she tried to put her finger on the other emotion that lingered in his haunting blue eyes.

She cleared her throat as she gave her head a experienced shake, trying to focus her now jumbled thoughts. "Roberto. Hi. I was just telling your mother…"

He stepped inside and crossed the room to open the refrigerator.

"That you were leaving. I thought you would be here for another day."

"I will, but I didn't think I would see you before I left so I asked her if she could tell you good-bye."

He poured himself a glass of orange juice, not bothering to meet her gaze. "I heard that already. Is that all you came here to tell me?"

He lifted the glass to his lips at the same time he fixed his penetrating stare on her.

Damn, why did he have to make this hard for her? He knew she owed him an apology and he was determined to drag it out of her, she glanced at Barbara in front of an audience no less.

"No, I also came to…."

"Hey, mom, whoaaaa, we have company," Brian said as he went into the kitchen.

Except for his dark hair, which she knew he got from his father, Roberto's older brother looked pretty much just like him with his classic good looks, adorable dimples, and piercing blue eyes.

He stood in his spot, looking down at her, so she smiled warmly and stuck out her hand. "Hi, I'm Diana Sanchez."

"Oh, shit."

"Brian!"

He ducked his head. "Sorry, mom, but she's that famous singer the girl Roberto used to like."

'Brian!"

Roberto's older brother shrugged, a mischievous grin lighting up his handsome face, when both Roberto and his mother called his name simultaneously.

"It's true. Did my brother tell you he used to talk nonstop about how talented you were back in school? Couldn't shut up. And now…"

"Diana and I need to talk alone. Excuse us." Roberto blurted out as he seized her wrist. Before she could utter a word, she found herself being tugged outside through the kitchen entrance that led to a huge tennis court.

Roberto seemed determined to put as much distance between them and his brother as he walked to the other end of the court.

He didn't stop until they were well hidden behind the large palm tree that blocked the view from the house.

"Sorry about my brother. He can be a little obnoxious."

"He wasn't obnoxious at all." She grinned playfully. "I didn't know you used to admire me."

She giggled before lifting her hands in mock surrender at the weakening look in his eyes. "Okay, okay. I was just joking."

She sobered then when she remembered why she was there in the first place. "Besides, I didn't come here to tease you. I came here to apologize."

"Go on," he said as he folded his arms across his broad chest and waited for her to finish.

She blew out a long breath as she went over the apology, she'd rehearsed in her bathroom mirror earlier.

"I consider you a friend, Roberto, and at one point you were my friend when no one else was. You have never been unkind to me, so I hope you can forgive me for what I said last night. I had no right to criticize the decisions you made.

From what I hear you're a damn good surgeon and…"

"A damn good architect, but you didn't know that did you?"

Her brows knitted together as she frowned.

"What are you talking about?"

A smug smile tugged at the corners of his mouth. "If you come back inside I'll show you. Oh, and you might as well stay for lunch. It's going to take you that long to finish eating your humble pie."

"Ugh, I'm an idiot," Diana complained as she closed her eyes.

"You said it not me. Would you like me to show you another award? If you give me a second, I can autograph one of my designs."

She glowered at him. "Are you done reveling?"

"Almost." He smirked.

She rolled her eyes before she returned her gaze to one of Roberto's bedroom walls that was entirely dedicated to his accomplishments as an architect.

Again, she criticized herself for having diarrhea of the mouth. Roberto had managed to not only live up to his parents' expectations but had also pursued his own passion for creating beautiful works of art.

He'd double majored in pre-med and architectural design in college and then earned a Master's in architecture while attending med school.

He'd gone on to design several buildings. Including the building that now housed his practice which he owned with his brother, as well as the surgical wing at the hospital where he'd completed his residency.

Diana felt like three times the fool. She'd been forced to sit through lunch while Roberto tormented her until they finished the meal, and then he'd shown her why indeed she would be eating humble pie for a long time.

She turned from the wall to face him, surprised that he was only inches away from her. When had he gotten so close?

Instantly, her body became aware of him, and she struggled to mask her physical response to him. She wanted Roberto to know that she had changed, that she wasn't the same over eager teenage girl who seemed like she was always in heat, but if she didn't get her body under control, she knew there would be no hiding the fact that his closeness was causing her internal thermometer to rise.

"I'm sorry Roberto for insulting you," she said quietly as she took a step back, but she didn't get very far when he snaked an arm around her waist and brought her body flush against his. Her lips parted and she stared up at him with wide eyes.

"You were wrong, so you owe me a kiss?" His eyes twinkled with mischief as his dimples popped out in his cheeks.

She gasped, recalling the familiar words he'd said many years before.

"You remember the last time I said those words, Diana?" He whispered softly, his voice wrapping her in warm velvet. She wanted to tell him that she would never forget what followed he'd said those words, but all she could do was nod. Her body was now on fire for him.

From the moment she'd locked eyes with him in the gym, her body had come to life as if it had lain dormant for fifteen years.

In truth, it had. No matter how many men she dated, she always compared them to Roberto and always found them lacking in some way.

He was never far from her thoughts and many times she'd wondered what would have happened to them if they'd had more time to explore the attraction that had developed between them all those years ago. He traced his thumb across her full bottom lip, and she shivered at his touch.

Then he lowered his head to press his lips against hers and her entire body instantly went up in flames.

Hot sparks of fire sizzled across her skin at the first brush of his mouth against hers. She moaned softly, opening her mouth to his searching tongue. She stroked her tongue against his, tangling it with his, sliding it into his mouth to taste him.

She moaned again when she tasted the exciting sweetness of his mouth. She loved the taste of him, the feel of him, hell, everything about him.

She lifted her arms to tangle her hands in his hair, holding him even closer to her.

She deepened the kiss, covering his mouth with her own as she drew his tongue further into her mouth and nipped gently.

He groaned at the same time he dipped his hands to her ass and brought her firmly against his hard length.

She instantly responded to his primal call as wet heat seeped from inside her to dampen her panties as her covering clenched and unclenched as if begging for him to slide his swollen length between her thighs.

She clung to him, her extremities wrapping around him like a twisted vine, pulling him deeper into her embrace.

She had no idea if they would have made love in his bedroom with his parents only a few feet away had his brother not burst in at that very moment.

At the sound of the door being thrown open, they separated. Brian glanced back and forth between them with a wide grin on his face, his expression unapologetic.

"You're such an asshole, you know that? You really need to get a girlfriend, or a dog, or something to divert your attention away from me."

Roberto complained as he straightened his clothing.

"Whatever, little brother. Dad and I need help outside and Mom want Diana to autograph all the CDs that you bought for her."

"Get out, Brian."

Brian ignored him as he turned his attention toward her, flashing her a hundred-watt smile.

"You know Roberto is infatuated with you. He's like your number one fan."

Brian never got the chance to finish when Roberto pushed him through the doorway and slammed the door in his face.

She grinned as Brian laughed all the way down the stairs.

"We better get downstairs before my parents send him back up here." She giggled when Roberto rolled his eyes. "My brother is an ass.

Nobody probably wants either one of us. He was probably just being nosy."

"Still, I better get going soon."

"Have dinner with me again."

She glanced up at him and the look on his face tugged at her heart.

She wanted to tell him that she had no desire to have a repeat performance of the disaster that was the tail end of their dinner date last night, but instead, she found herself saying just the opposite, much to her surprise.

"Why don't you meet me back at my hotel suite at 7pm? My treat, alright?"

She knew dinner, in her suite, alone. Was probably not a good idea, but she could not think of one reason to change their plans when he smiled and his tiny dimples creased his cheeks.

"Great. I'm looking forward to it," he said in a low voice, his eyes lingering on her lips, causing a slight tremor to race down her spine.

Before she could once again reconsider the wisdom of their dinner plans, he ushered her out of his room and followed her downstairs.

As soon as she got to the family's sitting room, she realized there was some truth to Brian's words. Barbara had indeed pulled out every one of her CDs and had them neatly stacked in a pile.

Laughter bubbled up inside of her when Roberto's mom held out a marker, a bright smile on her face.

"Mommmmm," Roberto shouted behind her.

She glanced over her shoulder and grinned at him. "It's fine. Go help your dad. I'll come say good-bye when I'm done. Go," she said with a firmer tone when he hesitated.

He let out a long sigh and shook his head, but not before he shot his mother a warning glance, as if to say don't bother her too much.

Diana glared at him until finally he got the message and just left them alone.

"I hope you don't mind, but I couldn't pass up this opportunity."

She turned back around to face Barbara and smiled.

"Of course, I don't mind. I am happy to autograph whatever you have."

She crossed the room and sat down on the couch beside the woman and signed each case with a personal note. She was about halfway through the extensive and complete collection when Barbara's unexpected words caused her pen to slip.

"I'm so glad that I finally got the chance to meet you in person. Roberto is a very guarded person, so I knew you had to be a very special woman to have had such a lasting influence on my son."

Her eyes snapped at Barbara's face, to meet the woman's probing stare. She felt naked under her knowing gaze, forcing her to let out a nervous chuckle.

"I think you got it wrong. It was Roberto who influenced me, not the other way around."

"He may have influenced you in the process, but it wasn't until after he got to know you that he found the courage to stand up to his father about his love for art.

He nearly gave Theodore a heart attack when he told him that he was going to double major in pre-med and architecture."

Diana shook her head. "But I had nothing to do with that. That was all Roberto."

Barbara lifted her lips into a patient smile. "Oh really? Then why did your name come up at least a dozen times during that conversation.

Roberto went on and on about how courageous you were, how you were committed to using your talent and not seeing it go to waste. How you had very little but managed to do so much with what you had…"

"He said that?"

She chuckled. "Oh dear. Over and over. That was just the beginning. He's one of your biggest fans and I know he's followed your career over the years."

She stared at her in disbelief. "Are you serious?"

"Completely. You left quite an impression on Roberto."

She snorted. "Yeah, I'm sure. Most likely the wrong one," she said as she rolled her eyes and resumed signing until the gentle touch of Barbara's hand against her arm forced her to stop.

"Diana, Bayside is a small town and it's not easy to keep secrets here." She instantly froze, recognizing the implication of the older woman's words. She narrowed her gaze, her eyes searching Barbara's face for the disgust she expected to see, so she was shocked when the older woman smiled, her eyes full of warmth.

"When Roberto became quite taken with you, I must say I was curious.

The person that other people painted wasn't the one that my son saw."

"The person that others saw was just as real as the one that Roberto saw. I just chose to show him another side to me, a deeper side to me," she said quietly.

"I disagree. I think the person you presented to my son was the real Diana," she said as she patted her arm and stood to her feet.

The older woman crossed the room and bent down to pull out a photo album from a bookshelf. Brushing it off, she walked back toward the couch and once again, took a seat.

"Diana, I try never to judge people on face value alone, because I of all people know that there is always more to a person than what we first see." She flipped open the album and ran a hand across several pictures that took up two full pages.

Curiosity filled Diana as her eyes roamed over the dated pictures before her that looked to be from the sixties. It took her but a moment to recognize Barbara and only a half second longer to recognize the familiar face of the woman who stood next to her in most of them.

The same dark hair, those same hazel eyes, and the same haunted look that used to burn in the depths of her own gaze, that a picture never failed to capture.

She gasped at the same time as she lifted her eyes to Barbara's face. "You knew my mother?"

Chapter 7

Barbara

"Dear, I didn't just know your mother. At one time long ago, we were best friends."

"What?"

Barbara sighed and closed the album, as she seemed to slip off to some faraway time and place that from the look on her face pained her to return to.

"Your mother and I knew each other from the time we were seven and we remained dear friends until the end of my freshman year in college, which was right around the time she met that no good father of yours.

I tried to talk her out of dating him, but she wouldn't listen and eventually we drifted apart. I returned to Bayside right after college, and by then your mother had turned into a person I didn't even recognize," she said sadly, and Diana knew she was speaking of her mother's addiction to drugs and alcohol that would eventually lead her into a life of prostitution.

She sat there in shocked silence, struggling to wrap her mind around everything as she stared at this polished and elegant woman who was so far from the woman, she knew her mother had been.

"Bitch but I got the impression that my mother was kind of wild in high school."

Barbara clucked her tongue against the roof of her mouth and grinned. "Oh dear, she was, we both were. Luella and I used to do everything we were told ladies weren't supposed to do."

"You? You and my mother? But you and my mother seem so.... different."

Her eyes were gentle as she clasped Diana's hands within hers.

"That's what I'm trying to tell you Diana. When I left Bayside for college I was a very different person from the one that returned. Some people accepted that, and some people didn't."

"Does Roberto know any of this?"

"Of course, dear. Kids can be cruel. I didn't want him to hear things about me from some kid on the playground. I wanted him to be armed with knowledge so that it didn't have the power to hurt him.

Granted, I didn't tell him everything. But he knew enough to realize that his mom was a very different person before she became his mother, and that that was alright, because as time passes people mature and they develop. Just as you have, Diana."

Diana was still reeling from the shock of the revelation that Barbara, the Barbara Cruz, had been a self-proclaimed "A demon" years ago. It seemed unbelievable. But Barbara had recounted tales about when she and her mother had been in high school that still had her ears burning.

The sound of a sharp rap against the door drew her attention and she glanced up from straightening a magazine on the coffee table.

Instantly, she pushed aside all thoughts of the wild women Barbara and her mother had been all those years ago. But she planned to revisit them later, she thought, as a smile crossed her face.

She chanced a final glance at the room service table, which was full of food, and then crossed the room toward the door.

Stopping to check her reflection in the full-length mirror one last time, with nervous hands, she smoothed her palms down her soft linen cream A-line dress with its scoop neck that gently hugged her curves.

She'd been going for sensual elegance and was happy to see she'd achieved it with the tasteful and flattering dress.

Satisfied that everything was in order, she finally opened the door. She should have been prepared for the overwhelming tide of emotions that always swamped her when Roberto was near, but as usual she wasn't. Dressed in a dark beige suit, he was breathtakingly handsome.

Her heart fluttered in her chest as she stepped aside to let him in. She'd been so focused on drinking in the beauty of his broad shoulders and muscular frame that it took her a second to realize he held a bouquet of red roses in his outstretched hand.

"For me?"

"No, they're for the bellman downstairs. I just brought them up here to see if you thought he would like them.

What do you think?"

Diana rolled her eyes as she took the flowers from his hand.

"Come in, smarty pants while I put these in water." She glanced back over her shoulder before she disappeared into the kitchen area of the suite.

"And thank you. They're lovely. I think the bellman would think so too, but I'm keeping them, so you'll just have to buy him something else."

He chuckled and she smiled at the rich quality of his voice as chills slid across her skin.

Damn, even his laugh was sexy. She put the flowers in a vase and set them on a table as she entered the living area again with a smile on her face.

"Are you ready to eat?"

He returned her smile. "Always."

She shivered slightly at the wolfish look he gave her when he spoke.

She got the distinct impression that at some level he wasn't just talking about food.

She did her best to ignore the undercurrent of attraction that pulsed between them as his hands brushed against her shoulders when he helped her into her seat.

She wondered again if maybe she'd made a mistake by inviting him to dinner at her hotel and not having dinner out at a public restaurant.

At the time it seemed like a good idea. She didn't want to chance running into more former classmates and face their judgmental scrutiny.

But now, she questioned whether she should have just taken the chance of running into them because they would have been far easier to deal with than battling her all-consuming attraction to Roberto.

"What are you thinking?"

Her gaze snapped at his face as he leaned back in his chair, studying her with piercing eyes the color of rich turquoise.

She smiled weakly. She didn't really want to tell him the truth, but she knew he was relentless if he thought someone was lying to him.

"That maybe we should have gone out for dinner after all."

He arched a single brow. "Why?"

She released a jagged breath, hoping he wouldn't be to put off by her honesty. "Because it's hard to ignore this thing between us when it's just us."

He quirked his lips into a lopsided grin. "This thing? That's what you're calling it?"

"What else should I call it?"

"How about attraction, longing, lust," he said quietly as he stood to his feet.

Diana's heart stabbed in her stomach as she followed him with her eyes. She thought he would cross the length of the table toward her, but instead he walked to the window of her room and stood before it, looking out over Bayside.

"When I discovered that you were coming back, I wondered what I would say to you," he turned around then to pin her with his gaze. "I wondered if the attraction we felt toward each other all those years ago was still there and if it was then what would it mean."

She stood to her feet and on shaky legs slowly crossed the room toward him, dinner long forgotten. It scared her to realize just how in sync she and Roberto truly were, even after all these years.

His words echoed the thoughts that had raced through her head when she made the decision to attend the reunion. What she felt for him all those years ago had not been imagined, but it was still there, and if it was then she too wondered what it meant.

She reached out one hand to press her palm flat against his hard chest, the steady thump of his heart pumping beneath her fingers. "And what do you think it means?" she asked softly.

"Since it's obvious that we're still attracted to each other?" He settled his hands against her shoulders and pulled her closer. Her next breath caught in her chest as she waited for him to speak.

"I think you know what it means, the question now is what do we do about it?"

She tilted her head back to meet his gaze and knew that the conflicting emotions that crossed his face were mirrored on her own.

"I want this, Roberto."

"I'm not just talking about making love, Diana. I want that too, But…"

She silenced him with a single finger to his lips. "I can't make any promises, my life is so complicated right now."

"You said that before and what did I tell you then?" He frowned at her and tried to set her away from him, his eyes full of disappointment, but she cried her fists, gripping his shirt beneath her tightened hands.

"I'm not going to let you walk away from me again. This time I'm prepared to give you all of me, but you must know that what you're asking for is very difficult for me."

"I know it is, but I'm not asking anything of you that I'm not prepared to give myself. I never was," he said quietly. The truth of his words was written right there across his face, and she didn't hesitate another moment as she lifted on her tiptoes, at the same time she reached up to grip the back of his head, pressing her lips against his.

The second their lips touched; her body ignited. She teased her tongue along his full lips until he parted them, allowing her access inside his mouth. Their tongues dueled as they kissed each other with a fiery hunger, and she poured all her pent-up longing for Roberto's in the heated kiss.

Without breaking the kiss, she slid her hands along his chest up to his shoulders and pushed his suit jacket down his arms until it fell from his body. Tugging at his tie she quickly discarded it before turning her questing fingers to his dress shirt.

One by one she undid the buttons of his shirt until it hung open.

She dragged her lips from his to drink in the sight of his hard muscled chest. Then with trembling hands she slowly pushed the dress shirt from his torso and just let it tumble to the floor.

She moved to reach for his belt buckle but stopped when Roberto seized her hands in his.

"Now it's your turn." He flashed her a wicked grin as his hands reached behind her to grasp the zipper at the back of her neck. He held her gaze as he inched it down until the flaps hung open at the back.

Then with achingly slow movements, he pushed the dress off her shoulders and down the length of her body until it pooled at her feet.

His eyes slid over her and she shivered under his heated stare. Her cheeks flushed with heat as she stood there while he drank his fill of her until finally his eyes returned to her face.

Then before she could take another breath, he hoisted her into his arms and carried her into the bedroom area of the suite.

With gentle hands, he laid her down onto the bed and she watched as he hurriedly undid his belt buckle and shrugged out of his pants. She gulped down a deep breath when he moved to join her on the bed, his hard erection tenting against his dark boxers.

She reached for him, and he settled his large frame against her as she held him within her embrace.

When he dipped his head to capture her lips in a kiss, she just sighed as pleasure unfurled in her belly and stroked its way from the top of her head to the tips of her toes.

Her hands roamed eagerly across his broad back as she slid her legs against his, enjoying the feel of his coarse hair as it tickled the sensitive skin along her thighs and calves.

He tore his lips from her mouth to trace a wet trail of kisses against the column of her throat, along her collar bone until he reached the upper swells of her breasts that spilled over the tops of her demi cup bra.

"Roberto," she gasped softly, her back arching off the bed when he cupped one breast in his hand and lowered his head to pull her erect nipple within the moist confines of his mouth.

He stroked her nipple with his tongue through the thin fabric of the white satin bra, and she tangled her hands into his hair, holding him tightly as he gently sucked and nibbled on her tender flesh.

He lifted his head slowly and stared down into her flushed face for just a heartbeat before he returned his attention to her breasts.

Looping his fingers under the skinny straps, he pulled her bra down her arms until her full breasts spilled forth.

A low moan exploded from his lips as his eyes fixated on the coral tips of her breasts before he once again dove back in to feast on them.

This time he worshipped her other breast as he nipped at her stiffened peak.

She closed her eyes and clung to him tighter as wet heat pooled at the center of her core, until she was writhing in pleasure against the bed, her juices seeping from her slit, to dampen her panties.

He continued to suckle at her breasts while he gently kneaded the yielding flesh until finally, she thought she would go insane.

"Roberto," she rasped out, her voice pleading with him.

"Tell me what you want, Diana. What you need."

"I need you."

He chuckled softly and then released her breasts to place butterfly kisses against her belly. He moved his way down the length of her body to dip his tongue into her navel before settling between her now parted thighs.

She lifted her head a fraction off the bed to meet his gaze.

"Tell me what you need, Diana," he asked again.

"You."

He grinned. "I know that but tell me what you need me to do. Tell me what will please you."

Her breath came out on a soft whoosh as the force of his words hit her square in the chest and despite all her efforts not to cry, she felt hot tears collect in her yes. For so many years she'd given to men, and they'd taken, but with Roberto it had always been different. He only took what he gave in return.

"Baby, what is it?"

She smiled as a single tear slid down her cheek. "It's just that I've never known a man like you," she whispered.

"You've always been so giving to me, wanting to please me, just so completely unselfish."

He smiled warmly, although his expression was serious, and his blue eyes sparkled with an emotion that was so overwhelming she had to draw upon everything inside her to keep from sobbing.

"That's how it's supposed to be, Diana. That's how it should have always been for you," he said quietly, and she felt another tear trickle down her cheek at the thought that she really didn't know what she'd done to deserve Roberto's affection, but she was eternally grateful that she had it.

He held her gaze for just a second longer as another intimate look passed between them, but then all thought once again flew from her head when he hooked his fingers beneath the thin elastic straps of her lacy white thong and tugged it down her legs until she kicked it off her ankles.

He once again settled between her thighs, his eyes burning with desire as he stared at her mound, which now glistened with her juices.

At the first touch of his lips against her wet folds, she cried out sharply, as shocks of heat sizzled across her skin.

"Oh, God. Oh God. Roberto," she moaned out, her thighs falling apart, and she gripped the back of his head as he devoured her cunt with his mouth. He parted her inner lips with his fingers and stroked two digits inside her, brushing against her G-spot as he sucked and nipped her erect bud, drawing the flesh deeper into his mouth.

Hoarse sobs bounced from her lips as she thrashed about wildly on the bed, but he didn't let up. He tugged mercilessly at her sensitive flesh, rotating the tiny nub between his lips until her legs began to quiver.

He shoved his fingers inside her repeatedly, increasing the pace as he pumped inside her tight flesh with deep stabbing strokes. She clenched her eyes shut, her hands grasping wildly at his hair as her pussy began to muscle spasm.

At the first wave of her climax, she arched fully off the bed, her toes circling against the sheets as she pumped her hips upwards, eagerly meeting the thrusting of his powerful fingers.

"Roberto! Yes! Yesssss!" She screamed out her orgasm at the same time sticky juices gushed from her spasming sheath to flood his mouth. She held his head firmly as she jerked her hips up to grind his mouth against her pussy as waves of pleasure coursed through her body.

Her body trembled around him for several long moments before the volcano inside her began to quiet.

"Ahhh," she sighed when the tremors from her orgasm slowly subsided and her limbs grew limp as she gradually relaxed back against the bed.

Roberto slid up her body, stopping only to first straw off his boxers and then to unclasp her bra from behind her, flinging them both to the floor in a messy mess where the rest of their clothes lay thrown about.

She sucked in a sharp breath when he finally settled on top of her, his hard erection pressing firmly against her wet hole. Hooking his arms behind her knees, he nestled his hips between her thighs but then held himself still.

She lifted her hands to his shoulders and stroked her palms up and down his arms loving the feel of his hard, bulging muscles beneath her fingertips.

She licked her lips as she worshipped his impressive form with her eyes before reluctantly dragging them to his face when he called her name.

"Diana, I need to ask you something and you must tell me the truth, okay?"

She wanted to scream at him 'right now' but just nodded her head in response.

"Has it been a long time since your last lover?"

She froze as she stared up at him suddenly feeling trapped. She didn't want to tell him the truth. Not now. Not when she was spread wide before him, naked, and already vulnerable.

"I need you to tell me the truth, Diana. I need to know that I'm not alone in this."

"You're not alone, Roberto."

"Then when was the last time you took a lover?"

Her heartbeat furiously in her chest as what seemed like endless minutes ticked by before she finally told him the truth.

"It's been two years," she whispered, letting her gaze slide away from him. "You were right all those years ago, what you said.

After my last boyfriend I didn't even bother dating anymore because none of them compared to you, none of them were you."

"You know your friends; they all think you're crazy."

Roberto lifted his head from his hands to peer over at Diana, a lopsided grin on his face.

"Yeah, I know."

She shook her head. "And you don't care?"

Roberto rested his head back on his hands as he lay stretched out flat on his back beside Diana, while they both stared up at the sky.

They were enjoying a quiet afternoon out at Bayside Lake to celebrate their high school graduation just days ago.

"Why should I? Their opinion doesn't matter to me."

"Yeah, well you know everyone thinks we're sleeping together."

A wicked gleam lit up his eyes and he rolled over to cover her with his body.

"Well, we both know that isn't true and why it isn't true so that's all that matters."

She twisted her lips into an abrupt frown, and he knew his nonchalant attitude was frustrating to her, but he simply laughed at the look on her face.

Later, he found himself laughing quite often, and he had Diana to thank for that. When she was with him, she let down her guard, and he'd discovered beyond music, she had a passion for literature, loved to play little pranks and enjoyed teasing him.

He didn't know what was going on between them, but he knew that whenever he was around her, he felt something that he'd never felt around any other person before.

He couldn't identify it, or describe it, but he knew he liked the feeling and that was all that mattered.

"Besides, I know you're just trying to distract me by changing the subject, but it won't work. You know you still owe me a kiss."

"What! That's not fair. You cheated."

"How did I cheat? You were wrong so you owe me a kiss."

She frowned at him. "You knew when we made that bet that you were already the class Salutatorian."

He grinned. "I told you my GPA was up there, but you didn't think a dumb, blonde jock could possibly be on the honor roll. Am I right?"

She gasped. "That's not true and you know it. Besides, don't act as if you didn't have your own preconceived notions. I saw your face when they called my name as a member of the National Honor Society.

Just because I didn't show up for any of those boring meetings didn't mean that I wasn't in it."

He ducked his head, as an embarrassed flush stole across his face. She was right. He'd been shocked when they called her name. But discovering that she was not only talented, but a gifted student as well, just further convinced him that he had been right all along.

There were many layers to Diana, and he had a feeling he'd only just scratched the surface. Now, he was more determined than ever to reveal each last one of them until he got to her core.

"You can protest all you want, but you still owe me a kiss."

"You know your GPA was only slightly higher than mine."

"Doesn't matter," he murmured as he dipped his head to brush his mouth against hers. He'd only intended for the kiss to be a gentle peck, but it quickly turned into something more when she clasped her arms behind his neck and parted her lips.

He eagerly swept his tongue between her lips to taste her sweet nectar. He could feel himself hardening as he rocked against her, pressing his erection into her belly.

He tore his lips from her lush mouth to bury his face into the hollow of her neck, while he skimmed his hands down the length of her body.

She wore a light summer dress, and he teased his hand along the edges, until he finally pushed it up to her waist, revealing her light-colored panties.

He stroked his tongue against her neck as his fingers pushed the scrap of fabric aside to probe the moist center of her pussy.

With one smooth stroke, he slid his middle finger inside her. She gasped softly and he groaned into her neck as her wet heat surrounded him. He stroked in and out of her, her cunt growing sticky with her juices as she twisted back and forth beneath him.

He raised his head for just a second to watch her. She was panting and twisting against the ground, with her eyes clenched shut, and her mouth slightly parted as she let out low moans of pleasure.

He stared transfixed by the sight of her in full arousal thinking she was the most beautiful sight he'd ever seen. He added a second finger and pumped inside of her, driving her closer and closer to climax.

He curved his fingers upwards, to stroke against her inner walls and brush her G-spot causing her to arch seductively off the ground.

"Roberto, please," she begged softly.

"Please what, Diana?" He whispered against her neck, delighting in the slight shiver that raced through her body when his warm breath feathered across the heated skin of her neck.

"Please make love to me."

He clenched his eyes tight as lust exploded in his belly. His cock pressed harder against the zipper of his jeans at her husky words. Damn, he wanted her, but he held back.

"I will, when you give me what I want."

"Roberto, please."

Despite the haze of desire that puzzled his brain, he could feel his anger toward her rising.

He pulled up from her so that he could stare down into her face and her eyes snapped open as if sensing the change in him. He held her gaze in silence as he tunneled his fingers inside her with brutal thrusts. She gasped and moaned out her pleasure, but she didn't tear her gaze away from his face.

"Give me what I want, Diana." His words were choppy as he quickened his already frenzied pace.

She shook her head, tears gathering in her hazel eyes. He slammed his fingers into her harder, his anger mixing with his burning need to bring her to orgasm.

"Why can't you give me what I need, Diana? Why can't you show me that I mean something to you."

Her breath hitched in her throat, and she struggled to speak.

"Roberto, but you do."

"Then give me what you've given no other man. Give me your...,"

"Roberto!" She screamed his name as she bucked wildly beneath him, her hips trembling off the ground to meet the pounding length of his fingers. Sticky cum gushed from inside her to coat his long digits as her body trembled wildly.

He didn't stop the rhythmic pushing of his hand until the final vibrations rocked her body.

Slowly he withdrew his fingers and while she lay completely spent beneath him with her eyes closed, he sucked her juices from them until he was sure her essence would always linger on his lips.

He stared down into her beautiful face, trying to memorize every single feature because sadly he knew this would probably be the last time, he saw her in person.

When he was sure he'd committed her image to memory he rolled over and collapsed beside her.

"I could make love to you, Diana, but tell me, what would make me different from other men? What would make me special?"

When she didn't speak, he glanced over at her, to see that she simply stared up at the sky, her face blank. He released a long, weary sigh as he stood at his feet.

"It's easy for you to give your body to men, but not your heart. Never your heart. Yet, the one and only thing that I want from you, you refuse to give, and that's not fair to me."

She sat up instantly. "What are you saying?"

He shoved a hand through his hair. "I can't keep doing this, Diana."

Her eyes widened as she opened her mouth to protest, but apparently glimpsing the serious glint in his eyes, she snapped it shut.

"The more time we spend together the closer we come to making love. Each time we go farther and farther and I'm afraid one day I won't be able to keep the promise I made to you and myself.

I am only human, Diana, and I can tell you it has been nearly impossible to stop when I've wanted to keep going."

"So, this is it, then. You're ending things."

His gaze roamed over her face, but there was nothing there, nothing but the stony mask she showed to the world to protect her from being hurt. The only indication that she was upset was the chilly tone of her voice.

"I don't want to, and you know this doesn't have to be over, but you have to give me something, Diana."

She twisted her face away from him, to stare out over the serene lake, and he thought it ironic that the lake should appear so calm when its visitors were going through such turmoil.

"I have given you more than I've given any other man before. Why can't that be enough?"

"Because if I accept what you've given me emotionally and then take our relationship to the next level, I know I will never discover the real Diana.

You refuse to commit because you're not ready, but I'm not sure I'm strong enough to keep this from getting physical until you are….,"

He let his voice trail off when she continued to stare out across the water. She was so frustrated! She was taking this as a rejection, but he wasn't rejecting her. Why couldn't she see that he was trying to do the right thing?

"Diana, I care for you, and I don't want to hurt you, but I am trying to show you that I'm not just like every other guy."

She whipped her head around to face him, her hazel eyes hard as stone.

"Just because you don't want just sex doesn't make you different.

You still want something. So, at the end, that makes you just like every other guy, if not worse, because unlike the rest of them, you want something that I'm not prepared to give."

He reared back in shock, not quite believing that she'd just said what she did.

Anger instantly exploded inside him, and he reached for her to drag her to her feet, his eyes blazing with fury.

"Don't you dare put me in the same category with the rest of those assholes. One day you will realize that what we share between us is special, because there are feelings here, and because we care about each other. But you will have to deal with the fact that you threw it all away because you were too afraid of getting hurt."

He dragged her flush against his body, his expression cold as he regulated his voice just above a whisper.

"But just know this, Diana, you're sadly mistaken if you think you can walk away from this completely unharmed and return to your old ways.

Because the next time you're with a man, you're going to feel different, empty even because it's hard to go back to meaningless sex once you've allowed yourself to care for someone. Believe me, that's exactly what it will be, meaningless."

CHAPTER 8

The Relationship

"What!"

The shock of her words had him spinning. He knew the reason why they were even there now was because she still cared about him, but he had no idea how much.

To realize that she'd been unable to have lasting relationships with other men because of her feelings for him left him humbled.

It also raised his need to claim her as his even more. The primitive man inside him just couldn't resist the desire to shout that she was his, always had been, and always would be.

She stared over at the wall as a red touch swept up from her neck to darken her cheeks.

"I know what you must be thinking. Two years? Believe me I tried to make things work with other men. But eventually I just gave up when I realized I always found something wrong with them simply because they didn't have your smile or your laugh or they weren't as chivalrous as you.

You were right all along. It felt so different just being in the arms of another man, that I just couldn't keep faking it. Everything about those experiences was meaningless because there was always something missing."

She shrugged. "Two years ago, I just got tired of being in pointless relationships."

He stared at her in astonishment. "So, you're saying you haven't Had…?"

She shook her head, her cheeks turning bright scarlet. "Nope. But I thought you knew that. I thought that's why you asked me how long it had been…"

"Baby, I wanted to know if you had a boyfriend. I asked you to make sure you weren't taken or spoken for in some way before I went any further. Now, I did suspect it had been a while, but certainly not as long as you…….wow."

"Ohmigod. I'm so embarrassed," she wept as she covered her face with her hands.

Gently prying her hands from her face, he leaned down to place a quick peck against her lips.

"Don't be embarrassed. Besides, while I didn't know it had been that long I could tell it had been some time since you'd had a lover…"

"How?"

A wry smile crossed his face. "I haven't forgotten one single thing about you, Diana. Not the taste of you on my lips. Not your unique scent. And certainly not the tight feel of your pussy wrapped around my fingers."

A dark flush spread across her face as she crumpled her lips into a tiny "oh" but then he pushed the tip of dick inside her and her expression took on an entirely different meaning altogether.

He was done with talking. They would talk later. Right now, he was more interested in claiming her and doing what he'd longed to do fifteen years ago.

He held her legs wide as he pressed forward slowly. She was still wet from her climax, but it had been so long for her that her muscles were firm as he pushed inside the tight walls of her cunt.

"Baby, you must relax. I don't want to hurt you."

She blew out a sharp breath as she struggled to open her passage to him by relaxing.

It helped somewhat as he worked the steel length of his hard cock inside her. He pressed forward until he was completely buried inside her, and the heavy weight of his balls rested against her soft flesh.

He pumped his hips slowly, as he gently worked his dick inside her until she began to stretch to accommodate him. Yet even after she began to relax around him, he still had to squeeze his eyes shut tight and concentrate hard on not embarrassing himself because she still gripped him like a tight fist.

Although, he knew instinctively that no matter how many times he stroked his length inside her she would always fit snugly around him because she had been made for him and only him.

He picked up his pace and drove into her harder and faster, tunneling his engorged flesh deeper inside her. His balls slapped furiously against her skin as the sound of sweat slick skin smacking together echoed off the walls.

"That's it Roberto, fuck me," she cried out beneath him as her hips matched the rhythm of his strokes, sending his cock thrusting deeper inside her until he swore, he brushed against the back of her cover.

More juice poured from her, soaking his dick it its wet warmth. He groaned as it seemed to seep through his skin causing his entire body to shiver with pleasure.

He shifted higher up her body, pressing her knees closer to the mattress as he slammed into her tight, wet sheath with wild, frenzied strokes.

His powerful thrusts drove the headboard of the bed against the wall with each thrust and for a fleeting moment he wondered if her neighbors would call the front desk and complain, but then her inner walls closed in on him and he lost all thought as he fought back the urge to spray inside her.

She was so tight, so unbelievably wet, and tight and he was close to losing it.

"Oh, shit, Diana. You must stop before I come."

"I can't. Oh, God. Oh, Roberto. I'm coming. I'm comiiinnnggg!" She dug her nails into his shoulders and threw her hips at him as she slowly came undone around him.

Violent shudders racked her body as her orgasm hit her and she bucked wildly beneath him.

He pounded his steel length inside her pussy, riding her hard through the endless moves of her climax. He was relentless in his driving need to brand her as his.

He draped her legs over his shoulders and cupped her ass with his hands, pounding her cunt with his cock until the last tremors of her orgasm caused her cunt to clench around him like a steel vise.

It happened so suddenly that he was unprepared for it and before he realized what was happening, he felt hot tingles of pleasure shoot from the tip of his dick straight to his balls and then he was coming.

He drove into her on one last powerful thrust, burying his cock inside her, balls deep. Seconds later, he roared out her name as jet after jet of milky white semen erupted from his dick to drench her tight walls with his seed.

"Diana! Fuck! Fuck!" He grunted loudly as he coated her sheath with his sperm until he felt as if he'd emptied his balls inside her.

He trembled above her as wave after wave of his climax crested and then broke inside him until finally, he could not hold himself up and was forced to collapse on the bed beside her.

Sweat beaded on his chest as he struggled to drag in normal breaths of air. When he finally was able to draw in an even breath, he turned his head to face her.

She met his gaze with a tentative smile.

He turned over to tangle his hand in her hair and placed a single kiss against her sweat slick forehead. He'd never thought this day would ever come.

Of course, he'd fantasized, but he never believed he would ever make love to Diana, the real Diana. The one who was open and vulnerable to him. The one who was able to emotionally connect with him.

He'd always wanted to hold this Diana in his arms and love her the way he'd always imagined, but he never thought it would ever happen.

His eyes snapped into her face at the soft touch of her hand against his cheek, but then every muscle in his body tensed when he glimpsed the look on her face.

"Baby, what's wrong?"

She smiled shyly, as an embarrassed flush pinked her cheeks.

"Uh, I think we forgot something."

He creased his brow into a frown. "What?"

"Um, well, I don't know how to say this…but I'm not on birth control and we kind of forgot protection."

He smiled as he rolled over to cover her body with his.

"I didn't forget it" he whispered.

Her eyes widened and he had to force himself not to chuckle at the laughable expression on her face.

"What!" She narrowed her eyes to study him closer. "Roberto, this is not a joke."

"I'm not laughing. Didn't you just tell me you weren't going to let me walk away again. You had to know that we were talking about something more permanent between us," he said quietly.

Her eyes grew wider, and in the next moment he let out a loud oompf as she pushed him off her and sat up, clutching the sheet to her chest.

"I thought you meant dating, not having a baby together!"

Sitting up, he placed a gentle kiss against her bare shoulder to soothe her. "I did mean dating and whatever else comes after that. We'll take it slow and get to know each other again."

She snorted. "That is if I'm not already pregnant."

"And if you are, we'll deal with that when the time comes." Sensing the storm of doubts brewing inside her, he wrapped his arms around her and held her tight in his embrace.

"Don't over think this, Diana. We've found each other again after all this time and I don't want to ruin this moment with doubts and worries."

He didn't miss the uncertainty in her gaze as she stared back at him, anxiously tugging on her bottom lip with her teeth. He cupped her cheek with his hand trying to reassure her not with words but with what he felt for her inside as he bared his soul in his naked gaze.

She hesitated for just a heartbeat longer before she tilted her lips into a tiny smile. The look that passed between them said so much more than what words could ever convey, and he had to restrain himself from shouting out loud at the depth of emotion he glimpsed in her eyes.

"You're right, it took us a long time to get here." she whispered as she reached out a hand to cut the back of his head. "And I don't want to ruin our time together either, so we'll save the worries for later," she said with a smile and tugged him toward her to press her lips firmly against his.

He groaned against her mouth as he pulled her up against him. Lying back down, he dragged her above him so that she could straddle his hips.

Another ragged groan escaped his lips when the sheet fell away from her body, revealing the lush beauty of her figure.

He ran his hands along her hips, across her waist, to settle at her breasts where he cupped their heavy weight in his hand.

He stared, excited by the beautiful jewels of her hardened nipples before he sat up to draw the stiff flesh between his lips.

"Roberto," she rubbed out as she gripped his head tightly. He feasted on her rosy tips as he moved between her ample breasts, lavishing them each with his undivided attention.

He could hear her breath coming in changing pants and he finally lifted his head from her breasts to stare up at her. Their eyes met and his heart nearly stopped at the combination of love and lust that blazed in the depths of her eyes.

His hands shook as he once again settled them against her hips. "Get on him," he growled out in a hoarse whisper.

She took his hardened flesh in her small hand and pumped gently. He sucked in a breath and closed his eyes as she worked her hand up and down his cock, stroking her thumb in the slit at the tip, to spread the drips of precum that gathered there across the head.

He groaned low in his throat as she stroked his dick, harder and faster, tugging at the sensitive flesh.

When she squeezed him tightly, he nearly shot off the bed.

"Diana, ride me, now. I don't think I'm going to last much longer," he croaked out.

She didn't hesitate. Moments later he thought he was going to die a slow death when she slid down on him, taking him inside her firm walls so slowly that he thought he would come before he could get all the way inside her.

"Oh, God, Roberto," she moaned out when she took the last inch of him inside her.

His chest lifted and his breathing became labored as he struggled to hold back his climax, when she began to bounce up and down on his cock, taking him inside her with rough strokes.

He held her hips as she slammed her cunt down on his hard length, the hot wet heat of her surrounding him like a warm, welcoming, tight cave, made just for him.

He groaned out her name when she quickened her pace. And he could tell she was close to coming as her thrusts down on his dick became wild and frantic.

He glanced up at her to see her head thrown back and her mouth open as she rode him at a frenzied pace.

He slid one hand behind her to cup her lush ass, while the other shot out between her legs to stroke her hardened clit.

"Roberto!" She screamed as she took him inside her with violent strokes. Her pussy began to pulse and vibrate around him, and he fingered the tiny core, harder and faster until hot, sticky wetness gushed out around his cock.

She cried out his name again as her orgasm roared through her. When her pussy clamped around him like a balled fist, he was powerless to stop his own climax.

On a loud grunt, he drove up into her with hard pounding thrusts, before he exploded deep inside her wet, tight warmth.

Pushing past her clenching muscles, he shuddered controllably as he emptied his seed inside her spasming cunt.

Vibrations continued to rack them both as she milked his cock with her warm pussy and jets of cum spurted deep inside her until they both had nothing left to give and she collapsed against his chest while he struggled to drag in a full breath of air.

He stroked her sweat soaked back for a long time until the sound of her even breathing reached his ears.

He glanced down into her face to see that she was now fast asleep. Then with them still locked tightly together, he too succumbed to a peaceful sleep, for the first time feeling truly content and at peace in Diana's arms.

CHAPTER 9

Diana

"Mommy, mommy, mommy!"

Diana smiled down at the raven-haired, blue-eyed girl that burst through the crowd in baggage claim to come barreling toward her.

Despite her expanding waist, she managed to stoop down and scoop her four-year-old daughter into her arms.

"Hi, sweetheart. Have you been a good girl for grandma and grandpa?"

Robbin shook her head, and Diana frowned as she let out an inward sigh, wondering what her precocious daughter had done this time to poor Barbara and Ted.

"I haven't been to grandma and grandpa's yet. Daddy said I could come with him to pick you up before the reunion."

Diana laughed as she placed a kiss against Roberto's forehead, her heart swelling with love for the daughter she'd conceived almost five years ago, to the day. She hugged Robbin tighter in her arms as she glanced over her head, her searching gaze skimming over the crowd that bustled along inside Bayside's tiny airport.

Her lips curled into a wide smile when she spotted him just a few feet away strolling toward her.

Good Lord, even after five years of marriage he still takes my breath away.

"Hello, gorgeous," Roberto murmured as he pulled her into his arms and kissed her with such a heated urgency that she feared she would catch fire right where she stood.

They would have stayed locked in each other's arms had Robbin not began to squirm.

"Daddy, I can't breathe."

He reluctantly tore his lips from hers, although his eyes promised he would finish what he'd started later before he turned his gaze to his daughter and plucked her from Diana's arms.

"I'm sorry pumpkin. I was just happy to see mommy," he said as he grinned at his daughter before he once again turned his attention back to her, his probing eyes searching for her face.

"How are you feeling?"

She knew what he was asking, and she smiled at the concern in his voice. "A little tired, but I'm fine and the baby has been quiet all night."

He wrinkled his brow as he shook his head. "I knew I should have put up more of a fight about you going to Rome."

She placed a single finger against his lips before he could launch into a lecture.

"It was only for a week, and this is my last trip so stop worrying, alright?"

He still wore a deep scowl, but she was grateful that he didn't protest further and simply nodded his head.

Even though she'd cut back significantly on touring, she knew he still worried that she traveled too much with her now being four months pregnant, but she'd tried to reassure him that she would never do anything that was beyond her limits or hurtful to their child.

She reached out a hand to stroke her palm against his cheek until his frown lines disappeared. "Are you ready to go?"

A knowing look twinkled in his eyes, and he smiled. "Desperately.

The sooner we can get to the reunion, the sooner we can leave, which means the sooner I can have you all to myself," he whispered close to her ear, causing a tiny shiver to slide down her spine at the thought of what awaited her later that night.

She returned his smile, clasping his free hand with hers. "Then let's go," she said as she walked with him and their daughter toward the parking lot. She couldn't wait either.

Diana straightened her dress from inside the stall for what felt like the hundredth time. She'd had to pee more times than she could count with the growing baby pressing down on her bladder.

Satisfied that her appearance was once again in order, she reached for the handle all set to twist the lock to the door and step out of her stall, but stopped when she heard her name.

An icy chill of fury settled over her when she recognized the voices that came from the other side of the door.

"I cannot believe he married that tramp. And now he's knocked her up again. Good God, men can be so dumb sometimes."

"Why is Roberto so dumb? It's obvious that he loves her."

"Oh, give me a break, Rebecca. Really, I don't know what he could possibly see in her.

He's probably after her money or something."

"Jessica, that's ridiculous. Roberto is wealthy in his own right. Besides, Diana is a beautiful woman inside and out. Can't you see that she makes him happy. Even back in school she changed him for the better after he started hanging out with her…."

Jessica snorted and she opened her mouth to say more, but Diana had heard enough as she barreled out of the stall, pinning the spiteful woman with a hard glare.

Jessica's eyes widened and she stared at her in shock as she backed away from Diana until she bumped up against the sink.

She struggled to hide her smile as she stepped around the trembling woman to wash her hands. She took her time, letting the charged silence stretch between them for several tense moments.

She finally turned her attention to Jessica as she was drying her hands with a paper towel.

She slid her disdainful gaze up and down the length of the woman, before she spoke.

"Jessica, as you can see, I'm pregnant so I'm not going to risk the health of my baby by getting upset with you because you're just not worth my anger. I will say this," she said in a chilly voice as she stepped closer to the woman to stand within inches of her.

"You can either keep my name from your lips or hope the next time you're insulting me and my family that I'm pregnant again, because if I'm not then I swear to God you're going to see the old Diana, and I can promise you that Diana will take great pleasure in kicking your ass just as much as she did back in high school."

She stepped away from Jessica to toss her paper towel in the waste basket, before leaning over the sink to check her lipstick in the mirror.

"Are we clear, Jessica?" She said icily, not even bothering to spare the woman another glance.

A small grin lifted the corners of her lips when the door banged shut behind the howling coward, she knew Jessica to be, with Rebecca at her heels, mouthing a silent apology.

She spent a few more seconds touching up her make up before she too left the bathroom. But as soon as she stepped outside, she drew up short when she nearly collided with Roberto.

"Are you alright?"

She smiled up into Roberto's worried face. "Of course, I am. Why wouldn't I be?"

"I just ran into Rebecca, and she told me you had a confrontation with Jessica."

"And as you can see, I'm just fine." She smiled sweetly at the skeptical look on his face, and then gently patted his cheek, before she locked his hand with hers.

"Jessica. Is she alright?" He said slowly.

She chuckled at the look on his face. "I'm pregnant, sweetheart. What could I possibly do to her?"

He narrowed his eyes as he studied her closely. "Diana, what did you do?"

"Why would you think I did anything? We're not in high school anymore." She grinned, her eyes dancing with mischief.

He pulled her closer as he shook his head. "Yeah, but in high school we had a principal, rules, and detention. There's nothing stopping you now," he muttered.

"You're right, but lucky for her I'm pregnant."

"Diana!"

She shrugged as a wicked grin curled her lips. "Hey. That's what reunions are for repeating old resentments, and reconnecting with old friends.

"She got on her tiptoes then to brush her lips against his before she said softly, for his ears only, and restore an old love that never died."

THE END

NEW YORK CITY'S GARMENT CENTER

Overview

The Creative Director of a high-end fashion label, Evelyn Torres, is a combination of brains and brass, who is an expert at spotting the latest trends, despite her own lack of style.

But another good thing she's good at spotting is players. So, when her boss hires Lucas Bravo as the VP of Acquisitions she is less than thrilled.

Although she accepted that he knows his stuff and is good at his job, he is nothing but a cavalier playboy who carries his good looks and charm like a weapon. But on a short business trip to New York, Evelyn comes to realize that maybe she was wrong about Lucas when he shows her that sometimes what happens in New York doesn't always stay there.

CHAPTER 1

Evelyn Torres

This was turning out to be the absolute worst day for Evelyn Torres's life. No. Take that back. The absolute worst day of her life was when Lucas Bravo was hired as the Senior Vice President of Acquisitions for the elite fashion designer label, the House of Fashion.

The only thing Lucas was good at acquiring were a string of model girlfriends, each successive one, more beautiful than the last.

"Signora Giordano, I really don't see why it's necessary for Mr. Bravo to accompany me," she said patiently, doing her best to her hide her irritation as she stared at Josefina Giordano, the elegant and beautiful older woman who'd built the House of Giordano from the ground up almost fifty years ago.

She'd worked for Giordano for nearly fifteen years, and she knew the woman didn't particularly like being second guessed, especially when she'd made up her mind about something, but she also knew Josefina was very reasonable. And she just happened to adore Evelyn, which in this case, was a check in her favor.

"Evelyn," she said, clucking her tongue as she gave her a sharp look. She knew then Josefina had seen right through her.

Hell, it was no secret that she could barely stand Lucas Bravo's guts. "I know you don't care for him, but he has a good eye for up-and-coming designers," she said with a slight shrug.

"Besides, he also has experience with swimsuit lines."

Well then send him, but without me! She wanted to shout, but since as far as she could tell she wasn't crazy, and she also didn't particularly relish the thought of standing in an unemployment line, she held her tongue and said instead, "I agree he is more experienced with these things, so he can just go without me."

"Evelyn!" She heard the warning in Josefina's voice, and she let out an inward sigh as she resigned herself to her fate, steeling herself for the lecture she heard coming.

"You're my Creative Director. Nothing comes in or goes out of my label without your approval. You're the only person I trust who shares my same vision."

She smiled then as a wicked gleam lit up her hazel eyes. "You know I would go myself if I didn't need to get ready for Fashion Week in a month. You may not like him, but you can't deny that Mr. Bravo is very easy on the eyes.

Who wouldn't want to spend three days in New York with such a handsome young man?"

Me! Evelyn silently screamed as she gritted her teeth. She stared at Josefina who wore an almost dreamy expression and shook her head, barely managing to keep her eyes from rolling to the back of her head.

What was with every woman that came within a mile of the man? Did he give off some deadly pheromones or was his cock just made of gold? Yes.

Lucas was extremely good looking, but he was conceited, cocky, and far too arrogant for his own good.

Why didn't other women see this?

Almost as if on cue, the man at the center of her thoughts strolled into Josefina's office with all the confidence and swagger of a man who knew he was practically irresistible to women.

Dressed in a custom-tailored charcoal gray suit that molded perfectly to his chiseled frame, he could easily have been a model with his sandy brown curly locks, great sea green eyes, and sun-bronzed skin.

He was just so classically handsome that it was almost nauseating. This time she didn't bother restraining herself as she crossed her arms over her breasts and rolled her eyes. She pursed her lips into a tight frown when she felt her pebbled nipples poke through the thin cotton of her dress shirt to stab her folded arms.

She swore he sensed his effect on her when he dropped his gaze to her crossed arms, before letting it leisurely slide back to her face.

Annoyance simmered in her belly when he flashed her a wolfish grin, and she rolled her eyes again before she snapped her gaze to a tiny spot on the wall just above Josefina's head.

"Evelyn. Signora Giordono," he greeted as he lowered his 6'5 "Hmpf." Was the only response she gave as her boss preened before him, soaking up his attention like a sponge.

She sat there in silence while Josefina went over the details of their trip to New York to scope out a few up-and-coming designers for a new swimsuit line.

Already knowing the rest of the talk, she shot to her feet, desperately needing to get out of the room now.

There was just something about Lucas that she swore whenever he was near the air in the room always changed, and her internal temperature seemed to kick up a notch.

"I have work to do, so I'll let you finish telling him what you told me, "She said to Josefina, who wore a slight frown, but when the woman didn't argue she took that as a sign that Josefina would let her off the hook this time.

Lucas instantly stood to his feet, and for some reason she resented his good manners and loyal ways.

Why couldn't he just be an all-around asshole? That would certainly make hating him easier.

"Evelyn," he said with a slight nod. "I guess I'll see you at the airport tomorrow. I must say I'm looking forward to working with you in New York."

There was something about the way he looked at her as he spoke that gave her pause and she narrowed her eyes, searching for the veiled come on that hovered just beneath the surface.

That's one of the reasons why she hated him so much. He always did little things to tease her and ruffle her feathers.

She stared at him for just a second longer, but if he'd meant anything more by his words, he didn't let it show.

She nodded toward Josefina, before she returned her gaze to Lucas.

"See you tomorrow," she said tightly before she twisted on her heels and stomped out of the room, desperately hoping her day didn't get any worse.

"I just prayed that my day didn't get any worse, but then here you come."

Lucas furled his lips into a grin as he walked into Evelyn's office, closing the door behind him.

He couldn't help but grin, although he knew it probably made her angry even more. His lovely Amazon reminded him of an angry scorpion always ready to strike.

He'd seen her cow many men who just couldn't handle her acid tongue and brusque manner, but as he drew closer to her, he knew instinctively that Evelyn was nothing but a little kitten under all that brass.

She just needed the right man to coax that kitten out of her.

"What do you want, Lucas?" She snapped as she leaned back in her chair with her arms folded across her full breasts.

He didn't even miss a beat as he let her brief words roll off his back.

"Just came by to give you the travel plan," he said, rattling a single piece of paper in his hand.

"You left before Josefina had a chance to give it to you."

He set the paper down before her as he planted both hands on top of her desk and leaned forward.

"You raced out of there so fast, you had me worried that you were about to miss your hot date."

She rolled her eyes. "You're the only one who has hot dates at ten in the morning."

"They're just dates, sweetheart; they're not hot to me at all."

He leaned closer to her then, his eyes drinking in her soft pouty lips, and almond shaped eyes.

"I'm just saving my time until I can convince a certain hot Creative Director to go out with me."

"Yes, well I'm sure your last Russian model girlfriend, ahhh, what was her name?" She cocked her head to the side as she stared up at the ceiling.

"That's right," she said snapping her fingers. "Nadenka. Yes, well, I don't think Nadenka would appreciate hearing that you don't consider her hot, especially after that blow job she gave you in your office last week," she mocked as she glared at him.

Irritation simmered in his gaze, as he glowered at her, struggling not to lose his temper.

"I already told you that she was on the floor looking for her contact. I was just about to get down there and look too when you walked in."

"Look, Lucas. Your sex life is none of my business. But just so you know, most women don't usually want to go out with men who change girlfriends as regularly as he changes his socks."

She dropped her gaze to her desk as she reached for the paper, he'd brought to her.

"Thank you for the travel plan, but unless there is something else, I really need to get back to work."

Just like that, he was dismissed. He stood there staring at the crown of her head, as fury whipped through his veins. She was barely civil toward him, but she'd never been outright rude.

For a year and a half, he'd been on the receiving end of her cold shoulder, and while he could take everything she dished out, that didn't mean he had to.

Before he stopped to think about what he was doing, he moved to the other side of her desk, and dragged her by her arms to her feet.

She stared at him openmouthed, her eyes wide. He knew the moment she regained her calm because her brown eyes darkened to tiny black chips, but before she could lash out at him, he beat her to it with his own cutting words.

"You're a real pain in my ass, you know that?" He ignored her gasp of shock as he plowed ahead, knowing she wasn't used to people talking to her in such a manner.

"You've been nothing but a bitch to me from the day I walked into your office. Don't you think it's time for you to stop?"

"I don't like you. I refuse to pretend that I do," she spattered out."

He narrowed his gaze as he studied her brown face, with her high cheekbones and full sensual lips, which was now marred by her angry expression.

She wasn't a model beauty, but she was lovely in her own way. Still, you would never know it with her severe bun, and librarian glasses. Not to mention her conservative, drab, power suits, which she wore like battle armor that hid what he knew was a killer body from the rare glimpses he'd caught of her in her tight spandex at the company gym.

At one time he'd wondered how she became the Creative Director of a couture fashion line given her own lack of feminine style, but after the one time he'd seen her in action, he'd never wondered again.

She had a observing eye, a calculating brain, and she could easily spot what would sell and what wouldn't.

With her superior intellect, she was one of those women who valued brains over beauty and power and hated anyone who used the second two to their advantage.

He had to admit that he wasn't afraid to turn on the charm to close a deal or charm a diva supermodel into doing a show, but he wasn't the male whore she thought him to be, and he was getting damned tired of having to always explain himself to her. Especially, when he knew the real reason why she lashed out at him, was not because she hated who he was and what he represented, but rather because she hated herself for being attracted to him, given who he was and what he represented.

"You say you don't like me. But I think it's the opposite."

"You're so arrogant that you would believe that but you're wrong."

"Am I?"

Later he would question what came over him, but the challenge in her words had him seeing red and he easily backed her up against her office wall, trapping her between it and the length of his hard body.

Settling his face in the crook of her neck, he stroked his tongue across her smooth skin that peeked out from just above her collar. He didn't mistake the gasp of pleasure that rippled past her lips, even as she made a half-hearted attempt to push against his chest.

He chuckled softly in triumph, stimulating a slight shiver from her body as goose bumps dotted the skin at her neck. "You say you don't like me, but I wonder if I stick my fingers beneath this skirt of yours will they find nothing but wet warmth."

"Lucas!" She gasped in warning when his hands began to tease along the hem of her skirt.

He groaned against her neck, as heat whipped across his skin and his cock hardened behind the zipper of his pants. The sound of his name on her lips was probably the sweetest thing he'd ever heard.

The teacher had set out to teach the student a lesson, but here he was getting schooled.

He knew then that if he didn't pull away from her now, she would wind up pinned down on top of her desk, with his cock buried balls deep inside her warm pussy.

He knew instinctively that the sensual woman inside her would wind up giving him the best ride of his entire life, but he refused to give into the temptation of fucking her.

She wasn't ready, and because of this she would end up resenting him for seducing her, even though it was he who was being seduced by her sensual attraction.

Pulling away from her, he held her gaze, as a myriad of conflicting emotions flashed across her face.

This was probably the first time she'd ever been forced to admit the truth of her attraction to him, and he was sure that inside she was running scared.

"You know I'm not the male gigolo you make me out to be, just as you know you want me, even though I'm sure you wish you didn't," he said with a wry smile, as he reached out to stroke his thumb across her full bottom lip.

"You also know that I've wanted you for a long, long time," he said in a low whisper. She started to shake her head, and while she hadn't parted her lips to protest, he still silenced the shake of her head with a single finger against her lips.

"There's no point in denying it. We both know the truth," he said firmly. "Do you want to know what else I know?"

He grinned when she shook her head again, but he ignored it. She probably didn't want to know at all, but he was still going to tell her.

"I know that when I take you for the first time, it's not going to be a quick fuck on your desk. I've waited a long time to get between your thighs, so believe me when I finally do, it will be in a soft bed, with soft sheets, someplace where we will not be disturbed because once I'm inside you, I don't plan to go anywhere for a very long time."

Her eyes widened in shock as she stared up at him, her mouth agape. He ached to kiss the sexy bow of her soft, succulent mouth, but forced himself not to as he dropped his hand from her lips and stalked out of her office, before he could conveniently forget all about those satin sheets and long lazy nights in favor of that hard, square desk.

CHAPTER 2

Lucas the Playboy

"How is it possible to have two back-to-back worst days of your life," Evelyn moaned as she stared in horror at the clothes in her suitcase. She was going to kill her best friend, Jasmine Mora.

She wanted to cry as she held up a pink, red top that dipped to a profanely low V in both the back and the front.

She had half a nerve to pick up the phone and curse Jasmine out for swapping out her conservative attire, for this trashy crap that her best friend called clothing.

Jasmine was lucky that she was exhausted from the long flight and too tired for a fight with her or else she would have picked up her cell phone and woken her ass up at one o'clock in the morning back in New York.

She should have known Jasmine would pull something like this when her best friend spent far too much time complaining about her casual outfits as she sat on her bed while she packed.

It all made sense now. She'd naively believed Jasmine had dropped by to comfort her after the run in she'd had with Lucas Bravo.

But apparently not. Apparently, the suitcase Jasmine had brought to 'spend the night' with was all part of her friend's grand plan to get her to "spice it up and cut loose while she was in New York."

"I'm going to kill you, Jazz," she vowed as she frantically searched through her suitcase only to discover more halter tops, ripped jeans, skimpy dresses, and stiletto heels.

Luckily for her, she'd brought a dress bag to carry her suits in to keep them from getting wrinkled, so she didn't have to worry about walking into her nine o'clock meeting tomorrow morning looking like some tacky tramp.

But tonight's dinner with Lucas was another story. If she hadn't agreed to meet with him tonight to go over tomorrow's agenda, she would have just ordered room service.

Tomorrow evening, she would head out to one of the malls on The Strip and buy some appropriate clothing, but since she couldn't wear what she'd worn on the five-hour plane ride out there, for now she was stuck with the slut gear.

Searching through her suitcase, she tried to find the least revealing outfit possible. It took her several minutes, but finally she settled on a pair of skintight holey jeans, a cream blouse, that was indeed see through but at least it had a built-in tank top beneath it.

She then pulled out a pair of cream and copper stiletto sandals with sequins across the toes to complete the outfit.

Dragging a hand across her face, she flopped down on the bed as she stared at the outfit she'd laid out. "This is a nightmare."

After the incident in her office yesterday, the last thing she wanted was for Lucas Bravo to see her dressed like a seductress.

With his massive ego, he would automatically assume her transformation was all for the purpose of attracting him, which couldn't be further from the truth.

Despite his words, and her body's false reaction to him and his damned heated words, she wasn't looking to become the next notch on Lucas' belt.

Men like him were a heartbreak waiting to happen, and she considered herself far too intelligent to be swayed by a hot body and a pretty face.

Standing on her feet, she resigned herself to her fate as she reached for the clothes on the bed. It was just one dinner, for no more than a couple of hours. She could handle that, but just in case she was wrong, she'd hit the bar before she headed into the restaurant and purchased herself some courage in a bottle.

Lucas passed by Evelyn's hotel room, as he walked down the hall of the Bellagio Hotel toward the elevators.

When he got out of the shower, he'd gotten her message that she wanted to play the slots for a few minutes and that she would meet him for dinner at their scheduled time.

He'd never figured Evelyn for much of a gambler, but hell, the casino was the place to indulge all your vices and fantasies if you wanted to.

At the thought of her, a slow grin spread across his face as he stepped onto the elevator. His normally acid tongue viper had been eerily silent on the plane ride over as she hunched in her seat, keeping their bodies as far apart as she could without flying through the window.

She was so transparent that it had been a struggle not to burst out laughing every time he glanced her way.

The events that transpired in her office yesterday had left her rattled and he figured the only way she knew how to handle everything was to just keep her distance. Her little strategies wouldn't work.

He'd spoken the truth yesterday; he wasn't some male slut chasing after one thing. Yes, he dated, but that was it. He hadn't taken a woman to his bed in over a year. Not that there weren't plenty that were eager to trip and fall on his dick.

Surrounded by models and fashion icons daily, he got his share of offers. But at thirty-eight, he was far too old to be bed hopping from one meaningless, faceless partner to the next.

Never mind, that had never been his thing even when he was younger. Yes, he was a charmer. Maybe that was the Italian blood in him from his maternal grandfather.

He enjoyed complimenting women just to see them smile, but there was a line between charming compliments and obvious flirting, and he didn't cross it. If Evelyn just opened her eyes, she would see that he flirted with her, and no one else, because he wanted only her. But after yesterday, he was sure there were no more doubts about that.

Still, even with his cards on the table, he knew she was going to be a tough nut to crack. He was up to the challenge.

As the doors to the elevator slid open and he stepped out, he kept that thought firmly fixed on his head, giving him just an extra pep in his step, as he strolled through the lobby on his way to Café Bellagio in search of the lovely Evelyn.

He passed by the casino area, the multicolored lights of the slot machines flashing before his eyes as the peal of endless ringing echoed all around him. He could easily see how someone could come to the Casino and lose it all.

The energy all around him was infectious and addictive, and if you weren't careful, you could quickly wind up bewitched by the magic of the city.

He maneuvered his way through the throng of people, the twinkling glow of the machines blurring his vision. He was almost past the casino area when he glanced over at the bar nestled in the corner. He quickly scanned the chic upscale décor of Yellow-Tail.

A regretful smile curled his lips then. Named after an Australian wine, the bar's name took on a whole other meaning if one just stopped to look at its patrons.

From the poorly clad women, to the undoubtedly married and taken men with their tongues hanging out and nothing but lust in their eyes, it apparently was the place to be if you were looking to get some "tail" for the night.

He wouldn't have given the place a second glance, had his gaze not zeroed in on a mocha hued woman with shoulder length caramel brown hair who was showing more skin than he'd ever seen her show in the entire time he'd known her.

He stood there rooted in his spot as he slid his gaze over her. She was almost completely unrecognizable, dressed in a pair of fitted jeans, with tears in strategic places, and a sheer ivory top that she might as well have been naked under, for all the good her low cut, mid drift baring tank top did to cover her lush, full breasts.

She sat at the bar, her fingers curled around the stem of an empty wine glass as she leaned into a good-looking middle-aged man, dressed in what Lucas knew to be a tailor-made Armani suit.

Jealousy whipped through him when she threw her head back and laughed at something the man said, her unbound hair brushing against her back. He had never once seen her laugh with such abandon, but here this stranger, whose eyes had not once made it to her face, was being treated to the sweet sound of her hushed giggle.

When the man's hand settled on her leg and began to stroke far too close to that secret place between her thighs, he lost it.

With angry strides, he brushed past any and every person in his way until he reached the couple.

With all the skill of a bull in a China shop, he sidled up to them and inserted his body in between them. He didn't even spare the man a glance as he glared down at Evelyn.

"Lucas! What are you doing?" She hiccupped.

He narrowed his gaze, taking in her flushed cheeks and dilated pupils. "You're drunk," he said flatly.

She flashed him a wobbly smile as she shook her head far too vigorously for her to be sober. "Not drunk. Tipsy. And you're being rude to my frrrriend." He frowned when she slurred that last word.

"Come on. I'm taking you back upstairs. We'll get some dinner from room service and see if we can sober you up." He reached for her then, but before her could grasp her arm the man who'd she been flirting with chose that moment to jump off his stool and position himself to his side, so that he had no choice but to go through him if he planned to get her out of there.

"Hey, the lady and I were having a conversation."

"Well, it's over. She's with me and I'm taking her back upstairs."

The man stepped closer toward him, forcing Lucas to size him up since it appeared he was going to have to fight his way out of there.

Just a couple of inches shorter than himself, the man was well built, and he knew that he may be a bit outmatched if it came down to brute strength, but if this old Casanova thought he would beat him because of his stocky build, well then he was sadly mistaken.

He wasn't leaving that bar without Evelyn, and he would take on ten more bodybuilder wannabes just like him if that was what he had to do to get her out of there.

"Yolanda never mentioned you. She said she was single."

"Well, she's not." He glanced down at the man's left hand, before pinning him with a hard glare. "Neither are you.

So, unless you want to explain to your wife how you wound up with a broken nose while on business trip, then I suggest you move."

The man couldn't disappear fast enough, apparently realizing that a one night stand wasn't worth the probing questions he'd have to answer later.

"That was rude. You're such a bully."

He turned around to face Evelyn, noticing that her hiccups had stopped. She looked like she was starting to sober up just a little, but she still had a long way to go.

Grasping her arm, he dragged her to her feet but let out a string of curses when she teetered tottered on her four-inch heels, forcing him to wrap his arm around her waist to keep her from falling.

"Why the hell are you wearing stilettos when you almost never wear heels?"

"They were the only ones that went with this outfit," she complained.

He rolled his eyes as he gave a quick shake of his head.

"Yeah, we'll talk about that outfit later," he grumbled as he hauled her against him and ushered her toward the elevator. Keeping his arm secured around her waist, he didn't release her until they were safely shielded in his hotel room and he'd lowered her onto his king-sized bed. She'd barely touched the bed before she flopped down onto her side.

"I think I'm going to be sick," she groaned.

"Serves you right," he muttered under his breath as he reached for the phone to order room service.

When he was done, he placed the phone back in its cradle and sat down on the bed where Evelyn was stretched out. She'd flipped over onto her back and had propped herself up against some pillows.

Although her hair was wildly upset, he could see the light returning to her eyes and knew that after she got some food in her she would be good as new.

Without a word, he stood to his feet again and marched into his bathroom where he filled one of the hotel glasses with tap water.

Walking back into the room, he held it out to her. "Thank you," she said weakly as she clutched the glass and drowned in the water. Three more times he did this until he was sure she was no longer dehydrated.

Once again, taking a seat on the bed, he nailed her with a hard look.

"What were you thinking going down there dressed like that and getting drunk? Were you trying to get taken advantage of?"

She shrugged, her expression defiant. "It's Vegas. I'm allowed to have a little fun."

He arched a single eyebrow. "Fun? That's what you call picking up strange men in bars?"

"I'm an adult, Lucas," she snapped. "If I want to get drunk and have a one-night stand, that's my business."

"That's what you were doing down there? Carousing for a one night stand when you knew I was on my way down there to meet you for dinner? Were you trying to make me jealous?"

From her shocked expression, he knew the thought had never even entered her mind, which infuriated him even more.

She had been down there on the prowl for men, but not to make him jealous at all. She'd been down there looking for a quickie affair, while he on the other hand had been up in his room thinking of how he wanted to spend these next few days doing nothing else but making love to her.

In one fluid motion, he shot out his hand and dragged her across his lap. She was so startled by the action that she didn't even struggle and he easily clamped his arms around her, imprisoning her in his embrace.

Still holding her trapped against his body, he lifted one hand to tangle in her hair, tipping her head forward, so that their lips were only inches apart. As if realizing his intent, her eyes widened, and she tried to pull away.

"Lucas, let go of—"

"If you wanted a male whore for a one-night stand, why didn't you just call me. After all that is how you see me," he said angrily before he crushed his lips against hers. He was so furious with her that it spilled forth in his kiss as he plundered her mouth with his lips. He didn't coax, he didn't tease, there was nothing gentle about the rough thrusting of his tongue as he claimed her as his.

Despite the anger that radiated from the kiss, she instantly responded, openly yielding to him as she arched into him, and allowed him complete access to the moist heat of her mouth.

With deft movements, he settled her on the bed and covered her with his body.

As some of his anger flowed out of him, his actions became gentler. He leisurely probed inside her mouth with his tongue as he tasted the sweet honey of her lips.

Twining her arms behind his neck, she groaned into his mouth, as she parted her thighs and rocked her hips upwards, to grind her pussy against his lengthening cock.

He dragged his mouth from hers and stared into her lust drunk face for just a second before he lowered his head to the crook of her neck.

Sweeping his tongue in the hollow space, he tasted her silky skin, dragging throaty moans from her lips as he pressed his bulging erection against her core.

He devoured her with his lips as he placed a trail of wet kisses along her throat. Grasping the hem of her shirt, he pushed it up her body and over her breasts, until he got it off her and flung it aside.

The succulent mounds of her full breasts spilled forth and he eagerly dipped his head to capture one stiffened peak between his lips as he massaged the other round globe.

"Lucas," she gasped, her back arching off the bed as she tangled her hands in his hair.

Swirling his tongue around one nipple, he tugged at it gently before nipping it with his teeth. Then he did it again until she was a writhing, screaming mass beneath him. But even after that he continued his sweet torture, lavishing her other nipple with the same undivided attention.

"Lucas, please," she begged from beneath him as she tugged at his hair, forcing him to lift his head to meet her gaze.

"I—I need you inside me," she said on a breathy moan. His cock, which was already hard, crushed against his zipper, straining to get out at her heated words. He ignored the demands of his body as he stared up at her face.

He didn't answer her, as he lowered his head to rain tiny kisses along her belly, at the same time he unzipped her jeans and tugged them, along with her black thong, off her body.

Tonight, he would give her the release she craved and prove to her what her body already knew. That she was his. But he wouldn't take her.

Not tonight. The alcohol mixed with her desire had left her horny. And as much as he hated to admit it, any man could have been between her thighs right now and she would have begged him to fuck her.

Lucas needed her to want him, not because she needed an itch scratched, but because her body hungered for him and only him.

He knew the only way she was going to get to that point, was if she opened her mind to the attraction that pulsed between them, which was something she hadn't done yet because she was still in denial that it existed as she fought tooth and nail against it.

But after tonight, there would be no way for her to deny it any longer. And he comforted himself with that knowledge as he lowered his head to stroke his tongue through the wet folds of her sex.

At the first touch of his tongue, she arched her back off the bed, as she fisted her hands in the bed sheets. "Lucas," she moaned, as husky pants tumbled from her lips.

He worked his tongue through the seam of her pussy, to encircle the tiny, hardened nub. Sucking her clit between his lips, he dragged her to the brink of ecstasy repeatedly as he tugged on it hard enough to bring her pleasure, but not enough to allow her to climax.

"Lucas, please," she panted softly, her voice catching when he stroked his tongue deep inside of her. Groaning against her soft mound, he inhaled the musky scent of her as he tasted her cream that gushed out from her hot center. As her thighs began to tremble around him, he felt his own body's response as he began to quiver.

Running his hands along her bare thighs, he devoured her with his mouth, drinking from her core as the evidence of her arousal poured from inside her. She writhed against the bed, and he glanced up to see her eyes shut and her face twisted in agony.

He resumed his sweet torture, as he gave her just enough to keep her hovering on the edge, but not enough to tumble over.

"Lucas, p—please. I need to come." The sound of her begging him for her release was almost his undoing. He had to draw in a deep breath of air to restrain himself from sliding up her body, freeing his aching cock, and giving her the orgasm, she craved with the hard thrust of his length inside her.

She cried out his name again as she grinded her sex against his mouth, desperate for the climax he held just out of her reach.

A soft low chuckle rumbled in his chest as her movements became more frantic more frenzied. Sliding his hands along the soft skin of her spread thighs, the soothing action seemed to quiet her restlessness as he finally gave in to her body's demands.

Closing his mouth around her clit, he tugged at the sensitive flesh, working it gently inside his mouth until he felt her shudder around him.

"Lucas!" She screamed as she tangled her hands in his hair and clamped her legs around his head. He held on as she rode his face, her hips pumping off the bed as her orgasm rocketed through her.

Her sweet, tangy juices poured from her sex, and he eagerly lapped them up until she had nothing left and she collapsed in a boneless heap against the bed.

He gave her cunt one final swipe of his tongue before he slid up the length of her body. Lowering his head, he captured her lips with his, and she moaned into his mouth, undoubtedly tasting herself on his lips.

He kissed her deeply, hungrily, his tongue probing inside her in much the same way he'd probed inside her sex.

He had no idea if he would have broken his promise not to make love to her that night, had room service did not pick that moment to knock on his door.

Twin groans of protest erupted from their lips as he slid off her and stood to his feet. He then covered her naked body with the comforter before padding across the room to accept the tray from the server.

After giving the man a tip, he closed the door and turned once again toward the bed expecting to find Yolanda twisted in his sheets looking like the sultry, sensual sex kitten he'd left only moments ago, but instead, he found her already half-dressed and looking to tear out of there like the devil was at her heels.

"What are you doing?" He asked with a frown, as he set the room service tray down on the table beside the bed.

Yolanda could barely look at Lucas as she hurriedly dragged on the rest of her clothes, struggling not to topple over in the stupid heels she'd worn.

Her brain may have been just a bit fogged from the five glasses of wine she'd had, but she wasn't drunk, which left her no excuse for what had just happened. She was so humiliated that she'd succumbed to the legendary charm of Lucas Gordon that she couldn't get out of there fast enough.

When she was fully clothed, she finally found the courage to meet Lucas' searching gaze, who now stood towering just above her. When had he gotten so close?

"Thanks for dinner, but we have a long day tomorrow and I really should be going to bed."

He stared at her, his eyes sharp, as he held her gaze. "So that's it? You're just going to run out of here as if nothing happened?"

"Yes, because as far as I'm concerned nothing happened," she said, moving to step around him but was forced to stop when he blocked her path. She glared up at him, to see his eyes flashing with fury as he stared down at her.

She sighed. "Look, Lucas. I'm sure you're used to women falling at your feet, but I'm not one of them, nor do I want to be. I was tipsy and a little out of it. Let's just chalk tonight up as one of those drunken moments and forget about it, alright?"

She could tell by the way his face hardened that he wasn't happy with her words, but there really wasn't anything else she could say. She wasn't trying to be mean, just honest. He enjoyed the chase, the need to conquer. This was nothing to him, except another conquest.

More proof of his expert skill as a lover. She on the other hand took the notion of intimacy more seriously and it was a blow to her pride to find herself being added to his long list of conquests.

Lucas didn't say a word as he stalked over to the table, grabbed the dinner tray, his back rigid as a board.

"Where are you going?"

"I'm walking you back to your room."

Yolanda nodded as she followed him, the tension between them thick and heavy as a midmorning fog, that she swore she would choke if she inhaled too deeply.

Neither of them said a word as they walked next door. Swiping the keycard, she unlocked the door and stepped inside, allowing Lucas to walk in behind her to set the tray down.

She felt she should say something to ease the tension between them as she glimpsed the tight set of his jaw and the cool, hard look in his emerald eyes.

"Lucas, I—"

"There is no need to explain yourself now. You were perfectly clear just moments ago." He dipped his head in a courteous nod as if they were strangers—as if his face hadn't been buried in her pussy just minutes ago. "Good night, Yolanda," he clipped out. And then he was gone as he stalked out of her room, slamming the door shut behind him.

CHAPTER 3

The Black Bikini

"Evita, can you take one last walk for us so that I can get a better look at the material?"

Yolanda glared at Lucas who stared transfixed by the tanned and gorgeous Brazilian model who'd already taken three runway passes in front of Lucas wearing nothing but a skimpy black bikini.

"Evita, we're done with you. Thank you," she snapped, a little shocked by the venom she heard in her voice.

Apparently, she wasn't the only one as she glanced around the room to see designer Leonora Vatrelli wearing a stunned expression, along with Evita. The only person who didn't look surprised was Lucas. He sat there wearing a self-satisfied smirk which she ached to slap off his face.

They were now on their third and final designer for the day, the third and final time she'd had to sit through a collection showing where he openly flirted with the stunning models while he basically ignored her.

She was jealous. Plain and simple. Just last night she'd told Lucas to get lost, so she shouldn't have been upset by his distance, but she was.

And she was furious with herself for the envy she felt, and more importantly, for letting it show.

"I seem to be feeling unwell so I think I will go." She said, shooting to her feet. "Leonora I will let Lucas finish up on my behalf." She had never done this. She had never been so unprofessional in her entire life.

As if remembering who she was, she flashed the designer a small smile.

"We are delighted to have you joining the team of designers at Dafina.

You really are an amazing designer, and your work is stunning," she said graciously before turning her attention to Lucas who stood beside her, his eyes full of concern.

"I'll meet you back at the hotel," she said quickly as she hastily tripped out of the small boutique with all the grace of a one-year-old learning how to walk for the first time. She heard Lucas call her name, but she didn't stop, she didn't even turn around as she rushed outside to Las Vegas Boulevard.

Within seconds she was hopping into a cab and tearing out of there to the Bellagio where she could nurse her wounded ego and bury her humiliation in the comfort of her private room.

He felt like an asshole as he stood on the other side of Yolanda's door. He'd openly flirted with a few of the models today, hoping it would make her angry. Although extremely childish, his actions had been harmless, his only goal being to prove to Yolanda that what they'd shared hadn't been just nothing.

Certainly not something to chalk up to a wild, drunken Vegas night and just forget.

He'd expected to get a rise out of her, maybe incite her temper.

What he never expected was to see the wounded look in her eyes before she sprinted out of there as fast as her legs could carry her.

He'd felt as if a knife was being twisted into his gut. In that moment he'd made a final decision about what would happen next between them. Enough of the games. They were too old to be playing them anyway.

Blowing out a long-ragged breath, he steeled himself for the onslaught of her anger as he raised his fist and knocked on her door. He deserved her fury. If she'd deliberately flirted with another man to make him jealous, he'd be pissed too.

He heard the door click as she unlocked it and he opened his mouth, wanting his first words to be those of an apology, but his words instantly stuck in his throat when the door swung open.

She stood there wrapped in a white velour towel with crystal droplets of water clinging to her satiny skin and her honey brown hair, hanging in loose wet waves to her bare shoulders.

"Lucas. What are you doing here?"

He crinkled his brow as he frowned. "You didn't even know it was me at the door. Is this how you open the door for strangers?" He said, as he raked his gaze over her.

"I thought you were housekeeping," she snapped, her eyes narrowing to tiny slits.

"Yeah, well, I'm not." He couldn't believe she would open the door in nothing but a towel and dripping wet even if it was housekeeping. In the back of his mind, he realized his reaction was a little irrational, but Yolanda had a way of raising his protective urges.

"May I come in?" She seemed to hesitate, so he added. "I need to go over tomorrow's schedule with you," he lied. He had no idea what was on the tomorrow's agenda, and he didn't care.

All he cared about was getting inside Yolanda's room so that he could figure out what was going on inside her head.

"Sure, just give me a second to put something on." She stepped aside to allow him entrance before she turned toward the bathroom.

Lust churned in his belly as he let his gaze trace the outline of her round ass and her long, silky legs as she walked away from him.

Letting out a low groan, he dropped down into a nearby chair and tried to erase the vision of Yolanda's long smooth legs wrapped around his neck, as he gripped her ass and road her voluptuous body all the way to paradise.

As if on cue, the object of his lustful fantasies chose that moment to saunter out of the bathroom, wearing a white terry cloth robe. He wanted to tell her that was only slightly more acceptable than the towel as his eyes drank in the sight of her creamy brown flesh peeking out from the V in the robe.

"About tomorrow. There are only two designers on the list so I…"

"Before we get to tomorrow, I want to talk about today." He interrupted.

Although she tried to hide it, he saw a tiny spark of awareness leap in her gaze, before she quickly masked it.

"I was tired, that's all."

Standing to his feet, he crossed the room and stopped in front her.

"So, you weren't jealous?"

"Jealous? Of what?" She said quickly, too quickly for him to believe she hadn't been jealous.

"I thought maybe you rushed out of there because you were upset with me for flirting with some of the models."

She shrugged as she waved her hand in dismissal. "That's ridiculous," she scoffed. "Of course, I wasn't jealous."

"And you expect me to believe that?" He asked in a hushed voice as he stepped closer.

"Look Lucas, you can believe what you want but…."

Her next words died in her throat when he reached out and dragged her against him. With one arm around her waist, he ran his free hand across her face, as his fingers gently stroked her luscious mouth.

"I apologize for trying to make you jealous. I did it to prove a point after what you said last night, but that's still no excuse. My actions were childish and stupid, and I'm sorry," he said softly.

She stood there her eyes wide with surprise and he wondered if it were his words of apology or the intimate way that he now touched her that had her in such a state of shock.

Tugging her closer, he held her body firmly against him as he dipped his voice to a low whisper. "I just wanted to clear the air. I don't want you to have any doubt that it's you I want."

He knew she wanted to say something, probably even protest, but he never gave her the chance when he lowered his head to press his lips against hers.

She knew he was going to kiss her, and she had plenty of time to pull away before he did, but she didn't. Instead, she parted her lips, allowing him access inside her mouth as she hungrily tasted him.

This was a mistake, kissing him, being alone with him in her room, but she couldn't find the will to push him away. His admission had taken her by surprise. She'd never expected him to acknowledge his behavior, let alone apologize for it. She'd also never expected him to accuse her of being jealous, but there was no point in denying it because they both knew the truth.

She'd been jealous. The only reason why she was even jealous was because she did indeed want him. Had for a long time, and apparently, she was just too tired to fight it any longer.

She'd expended so much of her energy pushing him away for so long that it was almost a relief to give in. In the back of her mind, she heard the protest that she didn't want to be added to this playboy's list of playthings, but she ignored her conscience.

Jasmine and Dafina were right. This was Vegas and she was with a handsome man who wanted to fuck her. Who the hell cared if he chased after everything in a skirt.

She deserved to have a little fun and if Lucas was providing it then who was she complained.

Twining her arms behind his neck, she held him closer, their lips and bodies fusing together as he backed her to the bed and pressed her deep into the soft mattress.

His hands roamed all over her, caressing and teasing as he stroked a small fire inside her.

She let out a soft gasp when he pulled away to stand on his feet. He smiled down at her. "I'm not going anywhere. Just getting a bit more comfortable."

His words didn't register in her brain until he began to unbutton his dress shirt. Her next breath hitched in her chest when he undid the last button and let his shirt fall to the floor.

Hard planes of muscle bunched beneath bronzed skin as he stood before her like a living Adonis. She could have died a happy woman with just that glimpse of perfection but then he unbuckled his pants, and pushed them down his thick strong thighs, revealing the most beautiful cock she'd ever seen.

She stared mesmerized by his stiff member, thick and long, as it jutted out from its nest of curly dark hair to point directly at her. She shuffled off the bed and lowered herself to her knees before him. He seemed to want to protest, but she never gave him the chance when she took his hard length in her hand and guided it into her mouth.

"Yolanda," he rasped as he slid his hand into her hair, to cut the back of her head. She closed her eyes, savoring the salty taste of his precum as it beaded on her tongue.

He was so large that it was impossible to take him all the way inside her mouth, but she easily set a rhythm, as she ran her tongue along the crown of his cock, while she gently massaged the heavy sacks between his legs.

She delighted in the sound of his harsh breathing as she took him deeper and deeper down her throat, her tongue drawing lazy circles up and down his length as she sucked gently.

He called her name again, his hand clutching her head tighter. There was something about the ragged moans that escaped his lips as he desperately said her name that sent heat pooling at her center.

When deep shudders began to jolt his body, she knew that he was close to coming, close to losing control and she worked her mouth faster, sucking vigorously as she did her best to take more of his large size deeper into her mouth.

"I'm about to come," he groaned as his hands gripped her head.

She felt him tugging at her hair, but she didn't relinquish her hold on him.

She would have eagerly finished what she'd started had he not pushed at her shoulders at the same time he drew back his hips.

"Not like this," he said in answer to the question in her wide eyes.

"I want to come inside you this first time," he said in a husky whisper as he dragged her to her feet.

Enclosing her in his arms, he once again claimed her lips in a probing searing kiss. Her body, which was already aflame, raged like an inferno as the heat of their passion consumed her.

She was lost so deep in the intensity of the moment, that she didn't realize he'd untied the belt around her waist until she felt the robe pool at her feet.

"Beautiful," he whispered reverently, and she lifted her gaze, expecting to see his eyes sweeping her body, but instead she found herself staring into his gorgeous sea green eyes.

There was something in them, an emotion that gave her pause and for just a second she hesitated.

"Lucas"

That's as far as she got when he swept her up into his arms, and gently lowered her onto the bed. Covering her with his powerful body, he settled between her parted thighs.

He held her gaze, his eyes conveying the intimacy of the moment, but he didn't acknowledge it, at least not with words.

Instead, he used his body as he pressed forward, the tip of his hard cock slipping inside her wet center.

"Look at me," he growled out when she closed her eyes. "Look at me as I enter you." She snapped her gaze to his face as she locked her legs behind his back and stared into his eyes as he pressed his thick length deep inside her, until he couldn't go any further.

"Oh, Lucas," she moaned, fighting to keep her eyes trained on him as her sticky warmth gushed out of her to coat his dick, easing his journey inside her tight passage.

Gripping his broad shoulders, she held on as he rocked gently, letting her slowly adjust to the size of him. But as she gradually stretched to accommodate him, he moved faster, sending his hard length tunneling deeper inside her.

Unable to hold his intense gaze any longer, she let her head fall back as she rocked her hips up off the bed, eagerly meeting his hard thrusts.

Hot shocks of pleasure whipped across her skin, with each stroke and she dug her nails deeper into his shoulders as the heat of her orgasm steadily built inside her.

It was as if he knew exactly what her body needed, as he surged harder into her, his pounding strokes faster and deeper. The sound of their sweat drenched bodies slapping together echoed in the room, as the musky scent of sweat and sex permeated the air.

The harder pace, caused him to drive deeper inside her and she felt lust clawing at her belly as she approached the zenith of completion "That's it baby. Come for me. Coat my cock with those sweet juices from your pussy." He slammed into her with brutal thrusts, the head of the bed banging violently against the wall with the force of their lovemaking.

Tears gathered in her eyes as he pummeled harder inside her, her channel tightening around him as the first tremor of her climax soared through her.

"Lucas!" She cried out as she jerked her hips off the bed, and finally did give in to the full onslaught of her orgasm as it erupted inside her.

As the muscles of her sex clenched around him, she felt Lucas' control snap as he plowed inside her on a final thrust, and then joined her in the euphoria of her climax as he exploded inside her.

The warmth of his seed flooded her insides at the same time he called out her name on a tortured roar of completion.

More wet heat poured from her cover, mingling with the evidence of his climax, as they both collapsed against the bed, their breathing labored.

Ignoring the crushing weight of his body, she kept her legs wrapped around him, as she gently stroked his sweat slick body until his harsh pants quieted.

"You have to let me go, if you don't want me to suffocate you." He chuckled.

"It's okay," she whispered, but she released him anyway, letting him tug her over to rest atop his muscled frame. Bracing her against his body with one arm, he pulled the comforter over them, as they laid there;

the distant hum of the crush of people and cars along The Strip was the only sound that floated into the room from the open window.

With her head resting against his chest, she closed her eyes and let herself be calmed to sleep by the steady rhythm of his heartbeat, as she pushed aside all the worries and doubts that she knew she would have to deal with, but she would deal with them later.

For now, she would just enjoy being in the arms of a gorgeous man who'd given her one of the most powerful orgasms she'd ever experienced in her entire life.

As she drifted off to sleep, she finally understood why women were obsessed with Lucas. If she hadn't experienced it herself, she would have never believed it, but yes, it was true. Lucas Gordon did indeed have a cock made of gold.

CHAPTER 4

"Where are you going?"

Yolanda glanced up from packing her clothes as Lucas ambled into her room dripping wet from his shower with a towel slung low on his hips. She released an inward groan as she stared at his chiseled body.

She wanted to scream at her pussy, down girl. They'd spent all last night and most of the early morning burning up the sheets, not to mention the two times they'd played the horizontal tango as soon as they got back to the hotel after their meetings.

"That's what I was trying to tell you last night, this morning, and as soon as we got back here, but you always have a way of distracting me,"

she said with a smile, before she turned her attention back to packing.

"Since we only had two designers today, I was planning to take an early flight back."

Crossing the room to stand beside her, his brows knitted together as he frowned. "Why?"

She pushed down on the suitcase until it clicked shut before she turned her full attention to him. "Because I have company coming into town tomorrow and I wanted to get a head start on cleaning up my place."

"I was hoping we could spend the rest of this evening enjoying Vegas." She heard the disappointment in his voice, and it tugged at her heart more than she wanted it to. This is just a meaningless affair, she chanted to herself.

This is just about sex, and nothing else, she forced herself to repeat over and over in her head, hoping it would stick, hoping that she didn't carry around this weight in her heart when she watched Lucas move on to his next conquest.

She knew what she'd gotten herself into, she just had to remind herself that she was a big girl having a grown-up affair. Hopefully one day soon, she'll believe that.

"I wish I could stay," she said with a small smile. "I've really enjoyed our time together, but now it's time to get back to the real world."

She swore he winced at her last words, but if he did, he didn't let it show for long.

"So how long is your friend staying? Maybe we could get together this weekend if you're not too busy."

Later she would realize that she was a fool, but she just wasn't used to having affairs, so admittedly she wasn't the best when it came to rules about what to say and what not to say. She ended up breaking the rule on what not to say.

"I imagine I will be a little busy, I'm afraid. Chris is planning to stay the entire weekend. He said his conference doesn't end until Sunday."

He arched a single brow. "Chris? As in a man?"

She may not have known the rules of having a fling, but she knew from the tightness around his eyes that she'd messed up.

Letting out a long sigh, she decided to just be honest.

"Yes, Chris is a man. He's my ex and he asked if he could stay with me while he's attending some mechanical engineering conference, he's in town for."

"I see." Several charged seconds ticked by as a tense silence hung between them before he finally spoke again. "You know when people come into town if they're there for the conference they usually stay at the conference hotel." His gaze bored into her. "I hope you know this Chris of yours isn't in town for the conference. He's in town to see you."

"I'd considered that," she said truthfully. And she had, which was why she'd made a point of telling him he could stay with her but all he was getting was a free bed, a couple of meals, and a very platonic friendship.

"I see." Was all Lucas said again as he moved away from her. A storm of conflicting emotions swirled inside her at the hard look on his face. She wanted to explain to him that Chris meant nothing to her, but then that would mean she'd have to admit that he did, and she knew Lucas wasn't that type of man. He enjoyed having flings, but that was it.

The only reason why he was even upset was because his ego couldn't handle the thought of her jumping from his bed to Chris'. But she knew that's exactly what he planned to do himself and she said as much.

"Look, I understand how this works, Lucas." No, she didn't. "We're both adults, we had an affair and that's that. I know when we get back to work it will be business as usual."

She was proud of the speech she gave, it made her sound sophisticated and worldly. As if she did this on a regular basis.

"I see." Was all he said again as he completely closed himself off from her, his face as empty as a blank canvas, devoid of any expression.

"I wish you would say something besides I see.

"What else is there to say? You seem to have this all figured out."

She heard the hard edge in his voice, but it only confused her more.

She didn't have time to figure out what was going on in Lucas' head. She had a plane to catch. "I don't know what your problem is. I would think you'd be grateful I wasn't trying to read more into this then there is. I just wanted you to know that I won't make things uncomfortable or weird for you back at work, that's all."

"How nice of you," he said tightly as he grabbed his clothes and stalked toward the door.

She didn't know what was bugging him, but she hated that he was leaving angry, especially after what they'd shared. If he'd been any other man, maybe she could have let her guard down, but Lucas was far too suave and sophisticated to open herself up to without winding up hurt.

"Lucas," she said quietly as his hand closed around the door. She watched him hesitate as if he wanted to pretend, he hadn't heard her and just walked out, but at the last second, he turned around. She didn't even recognize him as he stood there, his expression cold.

"I just wanted to let you know, I really did have a wonderful time," she said softly.

Something flashed in his gaze, but it was so fleeting that she didn't even have a chance to identify it.

In response to her words, he simply nodded his head and said with a tight smile. "Me too." And then he turned away from her and disappeared out of her room without another word or a look back.

She arrived yesterday evening to her apartment on ninety-fourth and third in the Upper East Side of Manhattan thinking maybe she'd misjudged Lucas. There was just something about his entire countenance as he left her hotel room earlier that day that made her question if she'd missed something very important.

It wasn't until the next morning that she realized she'd miss a lot, when a courier arrived, and she opened the package to discover the custom sea green box and classic white bow that identified the gift as one from Tiffany & Co.

A sense of dread gathered in her belly as she slowly undid the bow. She didn't yet know what was inside, but she had a pretty good idea who it was from.

Chris had never been particularly thoughtful when it came to gifts, or much anything else for that matter, which was one of the reasons why it hadn't been hard to let him go. He was now a good friend, but that's all he'd ever be. He was just far too selfish to be the man in her life.

As she tugged the top off the box and stared down at the beautiful bracelet, which sparkled beneath the rays of sunlight streaming through her window, she felt her heart skip a beat.

She appreciated the beauty of the signature Atlas bangle, but it was the card, and the inscription engraved on the inside of the bracelet that caused her next breath to catch in her throat.

How had she been so wrong about a man she'd seen every day for the last year and a half? How did she work side by side with the man and not get a glimpse of his true character.

Because you didn't want to see him as anything other than a wild playboy, a voice screamed in her head. She knew that voice was right, and she felt ten times worse because of it.

Lucas had tried to be as open and honest with her as possible, but she'd refused to allow him to just be himself. She'd refused to accept him for the man that he truly was. She was thirty-five years old and yet she'd never felt more foolish in her entire life.

Slumping down on her couch, she wallowed in self-pity for just a few moments before she realized that if she felt this bad, she could only imagine what Lucas was going through.

Reaching for her cordless, she dialed his cell, but wasn't surprised when it went straight to voicemail.

Instead of leaving a message, she hung up and dialed another number. The phone rang three times before a soft, familiar voice chimed out a perky greeting. "Hey girl. How was Vegas?"

Yolanda shook her head as a wry grin crossed her face. "I should shoot you for putting those clothes in my suitcase," she said, as she imagined Jasmine on the other end, twisting a shoulder length brown lock through her fingers, something she only did when she was guilty as hell.

"But did they work? You better not tell me you didn't get laid?"

She hesitated as she thought of Jazz's question, a wistful smile tugging at the corners of her lips. Yes, she'd gotten thoroughly and completely laid, no doubt about that.

"Oh shit! You did get laid! I knew it. I knew the clothes."

"Yes, I did hook up with someone while I was there."

"Who was it? Spill it."

She shook her head as she bit back a small chuckle. "It was Lucas," she said softly.

"Ohmigod! You didn't! You go girl. That man is fine, and I mean Fine."

"But Jazz, I think I messed up," she mumbled softly, cutting her friend off before she could steer the conversation in another direction.

"How could you have possibly messed up? It's sex. Don't tell me that hot man was bad in bed because it would be a damn shame."

"No. The sex was fine, better than fine," she said with a rueful smile.

"But that's not where I messed up." She told Jasmine the entire story, from the time their plane touched down up to now. When she was done there was a hushed silence on the other end before her friend exploded.

"Girl, are you crazy? You call Chris right now and tell his ass to stay at a damn hotel, and then you march up to LaGuardia and wait until Lucas' plane arrives."

"But I don't think he wants to see me right now." She hated the sadness she heard in her voice, but she couldn't help that her feelings we're starting to really show. She cared about Lucas, a lot more than she'd wanted to admit, but her feelings for him were impossible to ignore with this gaping hole in her heart.

"Oh, trust me. He wants to see you. But he's going to want an apology too. He went out on a limb for you, and you left him hanging.

You're going to have to grovel a bit for his forgiveness, but he'll come around as soon as he sees that you're willing to let your guard down with him."

She gently tugged on her bottom lip with her teeth, as unease stole over her. Jazz had far more experience with men than she did, but she still wasn't sure her friend was right about this.

"How can you be so sure he still wants me? What if I show up there and he blows me off?"

A derisive snort came across the line. "Honey, let me tell you a man does not buy a two-thousand-dollar bracelet for a woman he doesn't want and then have it engraved to boot. Girl, get your ass up and get it in gear.

There is a sexy man coming home in a few hours and you want to be the first face he sees when he arrives."

She listened as Jazz gave her more little tidbits of advice, before her friend had to end the call to get back to work.

"Thank you, Jazz."

"No problem, sweetie. Good luck."

She disconnected the call and sat on her couch feeling a million times better after the pep talk Jasmine had just given her.

As she sat there, it took her a few minutes to figure out what she had to do, but as soon as she did, she didn't hesitate. Shooting to her feet, she called Lucas again and this time she left a message. He'd put himself out there for her, and now it was her turn to do the same.

Lucas was exhausted by the time he got up to his office at eight o'clock that night. His flight had been delayed twice and the nasty turbulence had made it almost impossible for him to sleep.

As he let himself in, he trudged past the deserted cubicles toward Yolanda's office. All he really wanted to do was curl up in his bed and treat himself to a restful night of sleep. The last thing he wanted to do was go over one of the designer's portfolios on a Thursday night, with the last person he wanted to see. But he had to.

Dafina was expecting their report on her desk Friday morning before she left for a weekend trip to Paris that afternoon. She couldn't leave without that report if she was going to decide between the final two designers in time to start preparing for the Spring line.

In fashion, preparations for lines started months, sometimes years in advance, and they were already a month behind on the swimsuit component of the line.

They just didn't have time to spare, which was why as soon as he'd gotten Yolanda's message, he'd headed straight to the office without even dropping off his luggage at his home.

Seeing the light spilling over from under Yolanda's door, he knocked once before stepping inside. He knew something was up as soon as he walked in when he saw that she sat in her high-backed leather chair, with her back facing him.

"Lock the door please."

He twisted the lock in place, as he strode across the room.

"Yolanda, what is."

His next words died in his throat when she spun around in her chair to face him. Although the desk obscured the lower half of her body, he could easily see that she was nude as her lovely breasts winked at him, with their cherry topped nipples.

Despite his anger toward her, his body leapt to life. He wanted to scream at his lengthening cock that he was a traitor. He was still furious with Yolanda, but apparently his body didn't care.

"What are you doing?' He croaked out, slightly appalled that his voice cracked, making him sound more like a nervous teenage boy than the grown man that he was.

"I'm trying to apologize and seduce you all at once," she said with a naughty smile, although he could tell she was nervous by the wary look in her eyes. That's when he noticed the diamond and white gold bracelet that twinkled on her wrist.

"I see you got it," he said flatly as he frowned.

She nodded slowly. "I did. Thank you. It's lovely," she said with a small smile.

"I ordered it before you left." He added, as he tried to justify why he'd gone to such lengths to impress a woman who apparently still saw what she wanted to see and not what was in front of her face.

"I figured that. You had to have put in the order by the second day of our trip so the New York location could have it engraved and delivered by today."

He nodded, not knowing what else she wanted him to say. They both worked in fashion, so they knew how the process worked. She was right, he'd ordered it the second day they were there.

He'd placed the call right before he'd headed to her room to apologize, after their spectacle at Leonora Vatrelli's boutique, and if she thought more about it, it was also the night they'd first made love.

He'd called a friend at the New York location to get the gift rushed to her. In his mind he'd had it all planned out perfectly.

After they finished up on Wednesday, they'd have dinner, maybe go sightseeing or enjoy a show, before returning to the hotel where he'd planned to spend the rest of the night making love to her. And then when she arrived home the next day, she'd find the gift waiting for her on her doorstep.

His plan had never involved her flying home early so that she could spend the weekend with her ex.

"So, you got the bracelet, realized you were wrong and now you're here to apologize." He shrugged.

"Alright, apology accepted. Now if you don't mind, I'd like to go home and get some rest, since apparently this was just a pathetic ploy to get me to come down here."

He ignored the dejected expression on her face as he spun on his heels and stomped toward the door. At this point he was too angry to care. Why had it taken that stupid gift for her to realize what he'd been trying to tell her, show her, all along?

"Lucas, wait," she said, as she lunged out of the chair, and raced around her desk to clutch at his arm before he could walk out. He stopped to stare down into her face, valiantly struggling not to let his gaze drift lower because he knew if he did, it would all be over, and whatever she had to say would become secondary to his body's need for her.

And right now, he wanted to hear what she had to say.

"I'm sorry, Lucas," she said softly. "I didn't know how you felt."

"I've been trying to tell you all along." He thought of all the small overtures he'd made over the last year expressing his interest, only to be rebuffed. From the moment he met her, he knew that she would need a little coaxing, but he hadn't given up.

When the Vegas opportunity rolled around, he'd practically begged Dafina to send Yolanda on the trip with him, even though they all knew the job could have been accomplished with just one person.

"I realize that now, but at the time I just thought you were a notorious flirt and a gig."

"I know what you thought," he said dryly. "But those were your own issues, your own insecurities getting in the way. I never once behaved in a manner to suggest that I wasn't interest in you and only you," he said quietly as he lifted his hand to stroke her cheek.

"When it comes to men, I don't trust easily." He wanted to say he knew that better than most, but he kept his mouth shut as he just listened.

"Especially when it comes to men who are as handsome and confident as you." She lowered her gaze to the floor. "I just didn't believe a man like you would seriously be interested in a woman like me," she whispered, as she kept her eyes glued to their feet.

He swore softly as he dragged her into arms. He'd caught glimpses of this before, the insecurities that she carried around. He wanted to pummel whoever had convinced her she wasn't beautiful because she now seemed to believe it.

She was tall and curvaceous, and he often thought of her as an Amazon, toned and taut in some areas, and lush and full in others. She also boasted the most perfect features, with her pretty heart shaped faced, full sensual mouth, and alluring almond shaped eyes.

He'd been captivated the day he'd met her, and it had taken him awhile to realize she didn't see herself the way he did.

Sticking out a single finger, he lifted her chin until she met his gaze.

"Yolanda, you're beautiful. I've told you these many times before, as well as shown you with my actions."

She smiled. "I know. These are my own hang ups and I'm working on them." She reached up a hand to stroke his stubbled jaw. "I'm sorry it took me so long to see you for the man you really are and not the man I painted you out to be.

Please just give me the chance to show you that I see you for who you truly are," she said in a hushed whisper. "I know I don't deserve it. You've already done so much to show me how you feel and…"

He placed a single finger against her lips to keep her from babbling, something she only did when she was extremely nervous. He read the uncertainty in her gaze, as she searched for his face.

He understood her anxious expression, but if she truly knew just how long he'd been half in love with her, she wouldn't have been the slightest bit worried about his answer.

Yes, he'd been angry with the way things had turned out in Vegas, but he'd spent far too much time and energy pursuing her to be discouraged by a small bump in the road. He'd planned to return home, lick his wounds, and start fresh on Monday with her.

He knew when he'd started down this path that going after her wouldn't be easy, but then nothing truly worth having was ever easy to come by.

"Would it be corny if I told you that you had me at hello?" He said as he grinned down at her.

"Yes," she said with a small giggle.

"What if I told you, that you had me as soon as you turned around in that chair wearing nothing but a smile and my bracelet?"

"Still a little corny, but much better," she murmured as she twisted her arms behind his neck.

"You're a tough audience, you know that?"

Her eyes twinkled as red splotches bloomed in her cheeks. "Yes, but you love that about me," she purred softly as he backed her toward the desk, and she coiled one leg around his calf.

"Among many, many other things," he whispered before he dipped his head to capture her lips in a long sensual kiss. The urgency in his body belied the slow languorous kiss as he leisurely explored her mouth.

Sliding his tongue between her lips, he sipped from the sweet nectar of her mouth as his tongue stroked against hers and he gave himself over to the pleasure of melding his mouth to hers.

He tried to take things slow, but apparently sitting naked in a leather chair for however long she'd sat there had made her impatient as she tore at his clothes. She managed to rip his shirt apart before he once again seized control.

Flipping her onto her stomach, he bent her over her desk. Leaning his body over her, he whispered against her ear. "If you wanted me that badly all you had to do was say so. There are far quicker ways to get what you want."

He pressed the bulge of his erection against her ass, and he delighted in the shudder that coursed through her body.

With deft fingers, he unzipped his pants and eased his aching cock into his hand. Holding the turgid length in his palm, he pumped lightly as he slid the fingers of his other hand through the moist folds of her glistening sex.

Without warning he shoved his middle finger inside her and stroked it back and forth, eliciting a sharp gasp from her lips.

He slowly eased his digit from her creamy center, his finger coming away stained with her juices. He wasted no time in replacing the length of his finger with something far larger and more solid.

Gripping her full hips in his hand, he nudged at the dripping wet slit of her sex, stretching her slowly as he plowed inside her.

She moaned beneath him as she tried to rock her hips backwards, to take her deeper.

"You want this?" He whispered hotly as he held himself still. "Yes, please, please. Give it to me, Lucas," she begged as she twisted around to meet his lust filled gaze. Neither of them broke eye contact, when he surged forward, feeding her all his length on one single hard thrust.

Simultaneous groans rumbled from inside both, as their bodies fit together perfectly. Already he could feel his balls tightening as the muscles in her cunt squeezed around him. He knew neither one of them was going to last long as he stroked inside her on deep, hard thrusts.

He kept that pace for just a few seconds, before she reached out across the desk to grasp the other end. When she lifted onto her toes, sending him tunneling just that extra inch deeper, he lost it.

Palming her ass, he slammed his hard length into her at the same time he jerked her body back against him. His rhythm was frenzied as he fucked her with wild, primal thrusts.

"That's it. Fuck me Lucas," Yolanda shouted as her knuckles turned red from her death grip on the desk. There was nothing gentle about the pulsing rhythm of their bodies as they gave in to the demands of their desire.

He knew the moment her orgasm hit her, because he thought he would die when her cunt clamped around him so tightly that it was a struggle just to move an inch within her wet center.

Then hot, searing cream gushed out to coat his dick, and trickle down to his balls.

Somewhere in the distance he heard her scream several expletives mixed in with his name, but as the blood pounded violently in his ear, he was basically deaf as his own climax ripped through him.

He slammed into her repeatedly, his pace frantic as the slapping of his balls against her skin echoed in the room. It felt as if he thrust inside her a hundred times, but he knew it was just four strokes, before pleasure roared through him and he exploded deep into her waiting cunt, his warm, milky seed spurting forth to drench her inner walls with his semen.

He came for a long time as he dug his nails into the soft flesh of her hips, while their combined juices slowly trickled down her inner thighs.

With achingly slow movements, he pulled his softening length from inside her as he rested his back against her desk, struggling to drag in an even breath.

"What's so funny?" She asked when he chuckled softly beside her.

He turned to grin at her. "I just remembered the other day when I was in here. I fantasized about fucking you in your office, but I just knew I didn't want our first time to be on your desk."

"Well, you got your wish," she said with a twinkle in her eyes as she moved to stand before him, pressing her body within the wide stance of his legs as she twined her arms behind his neck.

"Yes, that was my wish, but not quite the position I'd imagined." He grinned as he placed a quick peck against her nose, wrapping his arms around her waist as he pulled her closer.

"Oh really? And what position did you imagine?"

In one fluid motion, he flipped her around and propped her up on the desk. "I kind of envisioned spreading your legs wide, pinning you down and fucking you hard atop your desk," he said hotly as he followed every description with the identical action, until she was laying spread eagle atop her desk, with his hands pressed in the crook of her knees.

"Well, I think we can fulfill that fantasy too, as well as many others,"

she said with a wicked grin as she held up her left wrist where the bracelet, he'd given her shimmered under the muted light.

"After all, I remember reading somewhere that Vegas was only the beginning," she said softly, reciting the words he'd had engraved on her bracelet, along with her name, as a dedication to her.

He smiled down at her. "The beginning of a lifetime," he said, adding another declaration, one he planned to make happen in the very near future.

He then lowered his head to press a gentle kiss against her soft lips as he gave himself over to the power of their passion, cherishing the thought that this was indeed the beginning of their lifetime together.

THE END

SPINSTERHOOD

ACKNOWLEDGEMENT

This novel is dedicated to my sister, Adelin Milagros Pagan Morales. There are no words to express how I feel about my sister. To me, she is just my guardian angel sent from heaven. Thank you, sis, for always looking out for me.

OVERVIEW

Spinster is a term referring to an unmarried woman who is older than what is perceived as the prime age range during which women usually marry. It can also indicate that a woman is considered unlikely to ever marry.

CHAPTER 1

The Origin of Spinster

Long before the Industrial Age, "the art & calling of being a spinster" denoted girls and women who spun wool.

Spinning was "commonly done by unmarried women, so the word came to denote" an unmarried woman in legal documents from the 1600s to the early 1900s, and "by 1719 was being used generically for 'woman still unmarried and beyond the usual age for it'".

As a denotation for unmarried women in a legal context, the term dates to at least 1699, and was commonly used in banns of marriage of the Church of England where the prospective bride was described as a "spinster of this parish".

The Oxford American Dictionary tags "spinster", meaning "... unmarried woman, typically an older woman beyond the usual age for marriage" as "critical" and "a good example of the way in which a word acquires strong connotations to the extent that it can no longer be used in a neutral sense."

By the 1800s, the term had changed to include women who chose not to marry. During that century middle-class spinsters, as well as their married peers, took ideals of love and marriage very seriously, and spinsterhood was indeed often a consequence of their loyalty to those ideals.

They remained unmarried not because of individual shortcomings but because they didn't find the one "who could be all things to the heart".

One 19th-century editorial in the fashion publication Peterson's Magazine encouraged women to remain choosy in selecting a mate, even at the price of never marrying.

The editorial, titled "Honorable Often to Be an Old Maid", advised women: "Marry for a home! Marry to escape the ridicule of being called an old maid?

How dare you, then, change the most sacred institution of the Almighty, by becoming the wife of a man for whom you can feel no emotions of love, or respect even?"

Currently, "unmarried woman" sense of the term in three ways:

(1) an old usage meaning "an unmarried woman of gentle family"

(2) a meaning related to but not tagged as archaic: "an unmarried woman and especially one past the common age for marrying"

(3) "a woman who seems unlikely to marry".

Dictionary.com describes the "woman still unmarried beyond the usual age of marrying" sense of the term as "Disparaging and Offensive". A usage note goes on to say that this sense "is... perceived as insulting. It implies negative qualities such as being fussy or undesirable". Also included is a sense of the word used specifically in a legal context: "a woman who has never married".

Wordreference.com describes the "woman still unmarried" sense of spinster as "dated".

Age is a crucial part of the definition, according to Robin Lakoff's explanation in Language and Woman's Place: "If someone is a spinster, by implication she is not eligible [to marry]; she has had her chance and been passed by.

Hence, a girl of twenty cannot be properly called a spinster: she still has a chance to be married".

Yet other sources on terms describing a never-married woman indicate that the term applies to a woman as soon as she is of legal age or age of majority.

The title "spinster" has been embraced by feminists like Sheila Jeffreys, whose book The Spinster and Her Enemies, 1985, defines spinsters simply as women who have chosen to reject sexual relationships with men.

In her 2015 book, Spinster, making a Life of One's Own, Kate Bolick has written, "To me, the spinster is self-reliant and inscrutable. We think we know what the wife is up to and what the mother is up to, but the single woman is mysterious. I like that mystery.

So, the term is a useful way to hold onto the idea of autonomy that can get so easily lost inside of marriage or motherhood".

In 2005, in England and Wales, the term was abolished in favor of "single" for the purpose of marriage registration.

However, it is still often used when the bans of marriage are read by Church of England parish churches.

Women may not have married for a variety of reasons, including personal inclination, a lack of eligible men and socio-economic conditions that is, the availability of livelihoods for women.

Social status issues could also arise where it was unacceptable for a woman to marry below her social rank, but her parents lacked the funds to support a marriage within their social rank.

In the early 19th century, particularly in England, women would fall under coverture, stating that all property and contracts in their name would be ceded to their husbands. This was particularly common in women who owned businesses.

The First World War, 1914–1918, prevented many within a generation of women from experiencing romance and marriage or having children.

In modern peacetime societies with wide opportunities for romance, marriage and children, there are other reasons that women remain single as they approach old age.

Psychologist Erik Erikson postulated that during young adulthood, ages 18 to 39, intimacy and a desire for isolation commitment.

Other reasons women may choose not to marry include a focus on career, a desire for an independent life, economic considerations, or an unwillingness to make the compromises expected in a marriage.

Some writers have suggested that to understand why women do not marry, one should examine reasons women do marry and why it may be assumed they should marry in the first place.

According to Adrienne Rich, "Women have married because it was necessary, in order to economically, in order to have children who would not suffer economic deprivation or social ostracism, in order to remain respectable, in order to do what was expected of women because coming out of 'abnormal' childhoods they wanted to feel 'normal', and because heterosexual romance has been represented as the great female adventure, duty, and fulfillment".

CHAPTER 2

Mr. Smith

Jose, my brother, would often get drunk when I was a little girl, but that put a different sort of fear in me from what Mr. Smith did.

With Brother it was a spiritual thing. Though it was frightening to know that he would have to burn for all that giggling and bouncing around on the stairs at night, the truth was that he only seemed jollier to me when I would stick my head out of the hall door.

It made him seem almost my age for him to act so silly, putting his white forefinger all over his flushed face and finally over his lips to say, "Sh-sh-sh-sh!"

However, the frightening thing about seeing my brother drunk was what I always heard when I slid back into bed.

I could always recall my mother's words to him when he was sixteen, the year before she died, spoken in her greatest sincerity, in her most religious tone:

"Son, I'd rather see you in your grave."

Yet, those nights got me very scared. That was clearly distinguishable from the terror that Mr. Smith filled by stumbling past our house two or three afternoons a week.

The most that I knew about Mr. Smith was his name. This I considered that I had somewhat fabricated by allowing him the "Mr.".

In my effort to humanize and soften the monster that was forever passing our house on Church Street.

My father would point him out through the wide parlor window in soberness and severity to my brother with, "There goes Old Smith, again." Or on Saturdays when my brother was with the Roman boys and my two uncles were over having hot cakes with Father in the parlor.

Father would refer to Mr. Smith's passing with a similar speech, but in a blustering tone of merry tolerance: "There goes Old Smith, again.

The rascal!" These designations were equally awful, both spoken in tones that were foreign to my father's manner of addressing me; and not unconsciously I prepared the euphemism, Mister Smith, against the inevitable day when I should have spoken of him to someone.

I was named Rita, after my mother. My mother had died in the spring before Mr. Smith first came to my notice on that late afternoon in October.

I had bathed at four with the aid of Lucy, who had been my nurse and who was now the upstairs maid; and Lucy was upstairs turning back the covers of the beds in the rooms with their color schemes of blue and green and rose.

I wandered into the shadowy parlor and sat first on one chair, then on another. I tried lying down on the settee that went with the parlor set, but my legs had got too long this summer to stretch out straight on the settee.

My feet looked long in their pumps against the wicker arm. I looked at the pictures around the room blankly and at the stained-glass windows on either side of the fireplace; and the winter light coming through them was hardly bright enough to show the colors. I struck a match on the mosaic hearth and lit the gas-logs.

Kneeling, I watched the flames till my face felt hot. I stood up then and turned directly to one of the full-length mirror-panels that were on each side of the front window.

This one was just to the right of the broad window and my reflection in it stood out strangely from the rest of the room in the dull light that did not penetrate beyond my figure.

I leaned closer to the mirror trying to discover a resemblance between myself and the wondrous Alice who walked through a looking glass.

That resemblance I was seeking I could not find in my sharp features, or in my heavy, dark curls hanging like fragments of hosepipe to my shoulders.

I supported my hands on the borders of the narrow mirror and put my face close to watch my lips say, "Away."

I would hardly open them for the "a"; and then I would contort my face by the great opening I made for the "way."

I whispered, "Away, away." I whispered it over and over, faster, and faster, watching myself in the mirror.

"A-way—a-way—a-way-away-away away." Suddenly I burst into tears and turned from the gloomy mirror to the daylight at the wide parlor window.

Gazing tearfully through the expanse of plate glass there, I beheld Mr. Smith walking like a cripple with one foot on the curb and one in the street.

Faintly, I could hear him cursing.

Presently, I was dry-eyed in my fright. My breath came short, and I grasped the black bow at the neck of my blue jacket blouse.

When he had passed from view, I stumbled back from the window. I hadn't heard the houseboy enter the parlor.

He must not have noticed me there. I made no move of recognition as he drew the draperies across the wide front window for the night.

I stood cold and silent before the gas-logs with a sudden strange memory of my mother's cheek and a vision of her in her bedroom on a spring day.

That April day, when spring had seemed to crowd itself through the windows into the bright upstairs rooms, the old-fashioned mahogany sick-chair had been brought down from the attic to my mother's room.

Three days before, a quiet service had been held there for the stillborn baby, and I had accompanied my father and brother to our lot in the gray cemetery to see the box.

It was covered with mud. In the living room, now by the gas-logs I remembered the day that my mother had sent for the sick-chair and for me.

The practical nurse, sitting in a straight chair busy at her needlework, looked over her glasses to give me some little instruction in the arrangement of my mother's pillows in the chair.

Just a few minutes before, the practical nurse had lifted my sick mother from the bed.

I had had the privilege of rolling my mother to the big bay window that looked out ideally over the new foliage of small trees in our side yard.

I stood self-consciously straight, close by my mother, a maturing little girl awkward in my curls and long-waisted dress. My pale mother, in her silk bedjacket, with a smile leaned her cheek against the cheek of her daughter.

Outside it was spring. The furnishings of the great blue room seemed to taste for that one moment of nature's life. My mother's cheek was warm on mine.

This I remember when I sat before the gas logs trying to put Mr. Smith out of my mind; but that a few moments later my mother indicated to the practical nurse and sent me suddenly from the room, my memory did not stay upon.

I remembered only the warmth of the cheek and the comfort of that other moment.

I sat near the blue burning logs and waited for my father and my brother to come in.

When they came saying the same things about office and school that they said every day, turning on lights beside chairs that they liked to flop into, I realized not that I was ready or unready for them but that there had been, within me, an attempt at a preparation for such readiness.

They sat so customarily in their chairs at first and the talk ran so easily that I thought that Mr. Smith could be forgotten as quickly and painlessly as a doubting of Jesus or a fear of death from the measles.

But the conversation took insinuating and malicious twists this afternoon. My father talked about the possibilities of a general war and recalled opinions that people had had just before the Spanish-American. He talked about the hundreds of men in the Union Depot.

Thinking of all those men there, that close together, was something like meeting Mr. Smith in the front hall. I asked my father not to talk about war, which seemed to him a natural enough request for a young lady to make.

"How is your school, my dear?" he asked me. "How are Miss Hood and Miss Herron? Have they found who's stealing the boarders' things, my dear?"

All those little girls safely in Belmont School being called for by gentle ladies or warm-breasted Negro women were a miserable sight beside the beastly vision of Mr. Smith which even they somehow fabricated.

At dinner, with Lucy serving and sometimes helping my plate, because she had done so for so many years, Brother teased me first one way and then another.

My father joined in on each point until I began to take the teasing very seriously, and then he told Brother that he was forever carrying things too far.

Once at dinner, I was convinced that my outrageous fears that Brother knew what had happened to me by the window in the afternoon were not at all ridiculous. He had been talking quietly.

It was something about the meeting that he and the Benton boys were going to attend after dinner. But quickly, without reason, he turned his eyes on me across the table and fairly shouted in his new deep voice: "I saw three horses running away out on Harding Road today!

They were just like the mules we saw at the mines in the mountains! They were running to beat hell and with little girls riding them!"

The first week after I had the glimpse of Mr. Smith through the parlor window, I spent the afternoons dusting the bureau and mantel and bedside table in my room, arranging on the chaise longue the dolls which at this age I never played with and rarely even talked to; or I would absent-mindedly assist Lucy in turning down the beds and maybe watch the houseboy set the dinner table.

I went to the parlor only when Father came or when Brother came earlier and called me in to show me a shin bruise or a box of cigarettes which a girl had given him.

Finally, I put my hand on the parlor doorknob just at four one afternoon and entered the parlor, walking stiffly as I might have done with my hands in a muff going into church.

The big room with its heavy furniture and pictures showed no change since the last afternoon that I had spent there, unless possibly there were fresh antimacassars on the chairs.

I confidently pushed an odd chair over to the window and took my seat and sat erect and waited.

My heart would beat hard when, from the corner of my eye, I caught sight of some figure moving up Church Street. And as it drew nearer, showing the form of some Negro or neighbor or drummer, I would sigh from relief and from regret.

I was ready for Mr. Smith. I knew that he would come again and again, that he had been passing our house for inconceivable numbers of years.

I knew that if he did not appear today, he would pass tomorrow. Not because I had accidental, unavoidable glimpses of him from upstairs windows during the past week, nor because there were indistinct memories of such a figure.

I hardly noticed, seeing him in the afternoons that preceded that day when I saw him stumbling like a cripple along the curb and beating and cursing the trees.

I do know that Mr. Smith is a permanent and formidable figure in my life which I would be called upon to deal with; my knowledge, I was certain, was purely intuitive.

I was ready now not to face him with his drunken rage directed at me, but to look at him far off in the street and to appraise him.

He didn't come that afternoon, but he came the next. I sat straight before the window.

I turned my head to the right to anticipate the sight of him and to the left to follow his figure when it had passed.

He was passing before my window, when I put my eyes on him and looked though my teeth chattered in my head.

Now, I saw his face heavy, red, fierce like his body. He walked with an awkward, stomping sort of stagger, carrying his gray topcoat over one arm; and with his other hand he kept poking his walnut cane into the soft sod along the sidewalk.

When he was gone, I recalled my mother's cheek again, but the recollection this time, though more deliberate, was dwelt less upon; and I could only think of watching Mr. Smith again and again.

There was snow on the ground the third time that I watched Mr. Smith pass our house. He spat on the snow, and with his cane he aimed at the brown spot that his tobacco made there. I could see that he missed his aim.

The fourth time that I sat watching him from the window, snow was falling outside; and I felt a sort of anxiety to know what would ever drive him into my own house.

For a moment I doubted that he would really come to my door; but I pushed myself with the thought of his coming and finding me unprepared.

I continued to keep my secret watch for him two or three times a week during the rest of the winter.

Meanwhile, my life with my father and brother and the servants in the shadowy house went on from day to day.

On weeknights, the evening meal usually ended with an argument between the two men. It was usually about the atlas or the encyclopedia. It usually took them towards the table to read out the statistics.

Often Brother was accused of having looked them up previously and of maneuvering the conversation toward the subject. The topics were very easily introduced and dismissed by the two.

Once, I was to send to the library to fetch a cigar. When I returned, I found the discourse shifted in two minutes' time from the Kentucky Derby winners to the languages in which the Bible was first written.

Once I heard the conversation slip, during a small dessert, from the comparative advantages of urban and agrarian life for boys between the ages of fifteen and twenty to the probable origin and age of the Icelandic parliament and then to the doctrines of the Campbellite church.

That night, I followed them to the library and beheld them fingering the pages of the flimsy old atlas in the light from the beaded lampshade.

They paid no attention to me and little to one another, each trying to turn the pages of the book and mumbling references to newspaper articles and to statements of persons of responsibility.

I slipped from the library to the front parlor across the hall where I could hear the contentious hum.

I lit the gas-logs, trying to warm my long legs before them as I examined my own response to the unguided and remorseless bickering of the masculine voices.

It was, I thought, their indifferent shifting from topic to topic that most disturbed me.

Then, I decided that it was the tremendous gaps that there seemed to be between the subjects that were confusing to me.

Still, again I thought that it was the equal interest which they displayed in each subject that was dismaying. All things in the world were equally at home in their arguments.

They exhibited equal indifference to the horrors that each topic might suggest; and I wondered whether their imperturbability was a thing that they had achieved.

I knew that I had got myself so accustomed to the sight of Mr. Smith's journeys, persistent, yet, moreover, seemingly without destination, that I could view his passing with perfect equanimity.

From this I knew that I must extend my preparation for the day when I should have to view him at closer range.

When the day would come, I knew that it must involve my father and my brother and that his existence, therefore, must not remain an unmentionable thing, the secrecy of which to explode now of crisis, only adding to its confusion.

Now, the door to my room was the first at the top of the long, red-carpeted stairway. A wall light beside it was left burning at night when Brother was out, and, when he came in, he turned it off.

The light shining through my transom was a comforting sight when I had gone to bed in the big room; and in the summertime I could see the reflection of light bugs on it, and often one would plop against it.

Sometimes I would wake up during the night with a start and would be frightened in the dark, not knowing what had awakened me until I realized that Brother had just turned out the light.

On other nights, however, I would hear him close the front door and hear him bouncing up the steps. When I then stuck my head out the door, usually he would toss me a piece of candy and he always signaled to me to be quiet.

I had never intentionally stayed awake till he came in until one night toward the end of February of that year, and I hadn't been certain then that I should be able to do it.

Indeed, when finally, the front door closed, I had dozed several times sitting up in the dark bed. But I was standing with my door half open before he had come a third of the way up the stairs.

When he saw me, he stopped still on the stairway resting his hand on the banister. I realized that purposefulness must be showing on my face, and so I smiled at him and signaled.

His red face broke into a fine grin, and he took the next few steps two at a time. He stumbled on the carpeted steps. He was on his knees, yet with his hand still on the banister.

He was motionless there for a moment with his head cocked to one side, listening. The house was quiet and still. He smiled again, sheepishly this time, and kept putting his white forefinger to his red face as he ascended on tiptoe the last third of the flight of steps.

At the head of the stairs he paused, breathing hard. He reached his hand into his coat pocket and smiled confidently as he shook his head at me. I stepped backward into my room.

"Oh," he whispered. "Your candy."

I stood straight in my white nightgown with my black hair hanging over my shoulders, knowing that he could see me only indistinctly.

I signaled to him again. He looked suspiciously about the hall, then stepped into the room and closed the door behind him.

"What's the matter, Betsy?" he said.

I turned and ran and climbed between the covers of my bed.

"What's the matter, Betsy?" he said. He crossed to my bed and sat down beside me on it.

I told him that I didn't know what the matter was.

"Have you been reading something you shouldn't, Betsy?" he asked.

I was silent.

"Are you lonely, Betsy?" he said. "Are you a lonely little girl?"

I sat up on the bed and threw my arms around his neck. As I sobbed on his shoulder, I smelled for the first time the fierce odor of his cheap whisky.

"Yes, I'm always lonely," I said with directness, and I was then silent with my eyes open and my cheek on the shoulder of his overcoat which was yet cold from the February night air.

He kept his face turned away from me and finally spoke, out of the other corner of his mouth, I thought, "I'll come home earlier some afternoons and we'll talk and play."

"Tomorrow."

When I had said this distinctly, I fell away from him back on the bed. He stood up and looked at me curiously, as though in some way resisted by me settling so comfortably in the covers.

I could see his eighteen-year-old head cocked to one side as though trying to see my face in the dark. He leaned over me, and I smelled his whisky breath.

It was not repulsive to me. It was blended with the odor that he always had. I thought that he was going to strike me. He didn't, however, and in a moment was opening the door to the lit hall. Before he went out, again I said:

"Tomorrow."

The dark hall and the sound of Brother's footsteps gone, I naturally repeated the whole scene in my mind and upon examination found strange elements present.

One was something like a longing for my brother to strike me when he was leaning over me. Another was his panic at my procedure.

Overall, I was amazed at the way I had carried the thing off. Now I only wished that in the darkness when he was leaning over me, I had said gracefully, "Oh, Brother," had said it in a tone indicating that we had in common some unmentionable trouble.

Then, I should have been certain of his presence the next day. As it was, though, I had little doubt of his coming home early.

I would not let myself reflect further on my feelings for my brother, my desire for him to strike me and my delight in his natural odor.

I had got myself in the habit of postponing such revelations until after I had completely settled with Mr. Smith.

As after all such meetings with my brother, I reflected upon the following punishments in store for him for his drinking and I remembered my mother's saying that she had rather see him in his grave.

The next afternoon, at four, I had the chessboard on the tea table before the front parlor window. I waited for my brother, knowing well that he would come and feeling certain that Mr. Smith would pass.

Because it was Thursday afternoon; and during the winter months I had found that there were two days of the week on which Mr. Smith never failed to pass our house. These were Thursday and Saturday.

I let my brother into that dull parlor chattering about the places where I had found the chessmen long in disuse.

When I paused a minute, slipping into my seat by the chessboard, he picked up with talk of the senior class play and his chances for being chosen valedictorian.

Apparently, I no longer seemed a mystery to him. I thought that he must have concluded that I was just a lonely little girl named Betsy.

I doubted that his nature was so different from my own that he could sustain objective sympathy for another child, particularly a younger sister, from one day to another.

Since I saw no favors that he could ask from me at this time, my conclusion was that he believed that he had never exhibited his drunkenness to me with all his bouncing about on the stair at night; but that he was not certain that talking from the other corner of his mouth had been precaution enough against his whisky breath.

We faced each other over the chessboard and set the men in order. There were only a few days before it would be March, and the light through the window was first bright and then dull.

During my brother's moves I stared out the window at the clouds that passed before the sun and looked at pieces of newspaper that blew about the yard.

I was calm beyond my own trust. I found myself responding to my brother's little jokes and showing real interest in the game.

I tried to terrorize myself by imagining Mr. Smith's coming up to the very window this day. I even had him shaking his cane and his derby hat at us.

The frenzy which I expected at this step of my preparation did not come. Some part of Mr. Smith's formidability seemed to have vanished.

I realized that by not hiding my face in my mother's bosom and by looking at him so regularly for so many months, I had come to accept his existence as a natural part of my life on Church Street, though something to be guarded against, or, as I had put it before, to be thoroughly prepared for when it came to my door.

The problem then, in relation to my brother, had suddenly resolved itself in something much simpler than the conquest of my fear of looking upon Mr. Smith alone had been. This would be only a matter of how I should act and of what words I should use.

From the incident of the night before, I had some notion that I'd find a suitable way of procedure in our household.

Mr. Smith appeared in the street without his overcoat but with one hand holding the turned-up lapels and collar of his gray suitcoat.

He followed his cane, stomping like an enraged blind man with his head bowed against the March wind.

I squeezed from between my chair and the table and stood right at the great plate glass window, looking out. From the corner of my eye, I saw that brother was intent upon his play.

Presently, in the wind, Mr. Smith's race went back on his head, and his hand grabbed at it, pulled it back in place, then returned to hold his lapels.

I took a sharp breath, and Brother looked up. Just as he looked out the window, Mr. Smith's hat did blow off and across the sidewalk, over the lawn.

Mr. Smith turned, holding his lapels with his tremendous hand, shouting oaths that I could hear ever so faintly, and tried to stumble after his hat.

Then I realized that my brother had gone from the room; and he was outside the window with Mr. Smith chasing his hat in the wind.

I sat back on my chair, breathless; one elbow went down on the chessboard disordering the black and white pawns and kings and castles.

Through the window, I watched Brother handing Mr. Smith his hat. I saw his apparent indifference to the drunk man's oaths and curses.

I saw him coming back to the house while the old man yet stood railing at him. I pushed the table aside and ran to the front door in case Brother was locked outside. He met me in the hall smiling weakly.

I said, "That's Mr. Smith."

He sat down on the bottom step of the stairway, leaning backward and looking at me curiously.

"He's drunk, Brother," I said. "Always."

My brother looked frankly into the eyes of this half-grown sister of his but said nothing for a while.

I pushed myself up on the console table and sat swinging my legs and looking seriously about the walls of the hollow hallway at the area of oak paneling, at the inset canvas of the sixteenth-century Frenchman making love to his lady, at the hat rack, and at the grandfather's clock in the darkest corner.

I waited for Brother to speak.

"You don't like people who get drunk?" he said.

I saw that he was taking the whole thing as a soared at his own behavior.

"I just think Mr. Smith is very ugly, Brother."

From the detached expression of his eyes, I knew that he was not convinced.

"I wouldn't mind him less if he were sober," I said. "Mr. Smith is like a loose horse."

This analogy convinced him. He knew then what I meant.

"You mustn't waste your time being afraid of such things," he said in great earnestness.

"In two or three years there'll be things that you'll have to be afraid of. Things you really can't avoid."

"What did he say to you?" I asked.

"He swore and threatened to hit me with that stick."

"For no reason?"

"Old Mr. Smith's burnt out his reason with whisky."

"Tell me about him." I was almost imploring him.

"Everybody knows about him. He just wanders around town, drunk. Sometimes downtown they take him off in the Black Maria."

I pictured him on the main streets that I knew downtown and in the big department stores.

I could see him in that formal neighborhood where my grandmother used to live, around Miss Hood and Miss Herron's school. Also, around the little houses out where my father's secretary lived and even in nigger town.

"You'll get used to him, for all his ugliness," Brother said.

Then we sat there till my father came in, talking almost gaily about things that were particularly ugly in Mr. Smith's clothes and face and in his way of walking.

Since the day that I watched myself say "away" in the mirror, I had spent painful hours trying to know once more that experience which I now regarded as something mystical.

The strict course that I, motherless and lonely in our big house, had brought myself to follow while only thirteen had given me certain mature habits of thought.

Lazy and wild daydreaming, I eliminated almost entirely from my experience, though I delighted myself with fantasies that I quite consciously worked out and which, when concluded, I usually considered carefully, trying to fix them with some sort of childish symbolism.

Even inactivity in my nightly dreams disturbed me. Sometimes as I tossed half-awake in my big bed, I would try to piece together my dreams into at least one form of logic.

Sometimes I would complete an unfinished dream and wouldn't know in the morning what part I had dreamed and what part was pieced out.

I would often smile over the ends that I had plotted in half wakeful moments but found pride in dreams that were complete in themselves and easy to fix with symbol, which I called "meaning."

I found that a dream could start for no discoverable reason, with the sight of a printed page on which the first line was, "Once upon a time"; and soon could have me a character in a strange story.

Once upon a time there was a little girl whose hands began to get very large. Grown men came for miles around to look at the giant hands and to shake them, but the little girl was ashamed of them and hid them under her skirt.

It seemed that the little girl lived in the stable behind my grandmother's old house, and I watched her from the top of the loft ladder.

Whenever there was the sound of footsteps, she trembled and wept; so, I would beat on the floor above her and laugh uproariously at her fear.

Presently, I am the little girl listening to the noise. At first, I trembled and called out for my father, but then I recollected that it was I who had made the noises and I felt that I had made a very considerable discovery for myself.

I woke up one Saturday morning in early March to the sound of my father's voice in the downstairs hall. He was talking to the servants, ordering the carriage, I think.

I believe that I awoke at the sound of the carriage horses' names. I went to my door and called "good-bye" to him.

He was twisting his mustache before the hall mirror, and he looked up the stairway at me and smiled.

He was always abashed to be caught before a looking-glass, and he called out self-consciously and affectionately that he would be home at noon.

I closed my door and went to the little dressing table that he had put in my room on my birthday.

The card with his handwriting on it was still stuck in the corner of the mirror: "For my young lady daughter."

I was so thoroughly aware of the gentleness in his nature this morning that any childish timidity before him would, I thought, seem an injustice, and I determined that I should sit with him and my uncles in the parlor that afternoon and perhaps tell them all my fear of the habitually drunken Mr. Smith and with them watch him pass before the parlor window.

That morning I sat before the mirror of my dressing table and put up my hair in a knot on the back of my head for the first time.

Before Father came home at noon, however, I had taken my hair down, and I was not now certain that he would be unoffended by my mention of the neighborhood drunkard.

I was resolute in my purpose, and when my two uncles came after lunch, and the three men shut themselves up in the parlor for the afternoon, I took my seat across the hall in the little library, or den, as my mother had called it, and spent the first of the afternoon skimming over the familiar pages of Tales of Ol' Virginny, by Thomas Nelson Page.

My father seemed tired at lunch. He talked very little and drank only half his cup of coffee. He asked Brother matter-of-fact questions about his plans for college in the fall and told me once to try cutting my meat instead of pulling it to pieces.

As I sat in the library afterward, I wondered if he had been thinking of my mother.

Indeed, I wondered whether he ever thought of her. He never mentioned her to us; and in a year I had forgotten exactly how he treated her when she had been alive.

It was not only the fate of my brother's soul that I had given thought to since my mother's death.

Father had always had his whiskey on Saturday afternoon with his two bachelor brothers. There was more than one round served in the parlor on Saturday now.

Throughout the early part of this afternoon, I could hear the tinkle of the bell in the kitchen, and presently the houseboy would appear at the door of the parlor with a tray of ice-filled glasses.

As he entered the parlor each time, I would catch a glimpse over my book of the three men. One was usually standing; whichever one was leading the conversation. Once they were laughing heartily; and as the

Negro boy came out with the tray of empty glasses, there was a smile on his face.

As their voices grew louder and merrier, my courage relaxed. It was then I first put into words the thought that in my brother and father I saw something of Mr. Smith. I knew that it was more than a taste of whisky they had in common.

At four o'clock I heard Brother's voice mixed with those of the Benton boys outside the front door.

They came into the hall, and their voices were high and excited. First one, then another would demand to be heard with: "No, listen now; let me tell you what."

In just a few minutes, I heard Brother on the stairs. Then two of the Benton brothers appeared in t the doorway of the library. Even the youngest, who was not a year older than I and whose name was Henry, wore long pants, and each carried a cap in hand and a linen duster over his arm.

I stood up and smiled at them, and with my right forefinger I pushed the black locks which hung loosely about my shoulders behind my ears.

"We're going motoring in the Carltons' machine," Henry said.

I stammered in surprise and asked if Brother was going to ride in it. One of them said that he was upstairs getting his hunting cap, since he had no motoring cap. The older brother, Gary Benton, went back into the hall. I walked toward Henry, who was standing in the doorway.

"But does Father know you're going?" I asked.

As I tried to go through the doorway, Henry stretched his arm across it and looked at me with a critical frown on his face.

"Why don't you put up your hair?" he said.

I looked at him seriously, and I felt the heat of the blush that came over my face. I felt it on the back of my neck.

I stooped with what I thought considerable grace and slid under his arm and passed into the hall.

There were the other two Benton boys listening to the voices of my uncles and my father through the parlor door.

I stepped between them and threw open the door. Just as I did so, Henry Benton commanded, "Elizabeth, don't do that!" I was swinging the door open, turned, and smiled at him.

I stood for a moment looking blandly at my father and my uncles. I was considering what had made me burst in upon them in this manner.

It was not merely that I had perceived the opportunity of creating this little disturbance and slipping in under its noise, though I was not unaware of the advantage.

I was frightened by the boys' threatening adventure in the horseless carriage but surely not so much as I normally should have been at breaking into the parlor at this forbidden hour.

The immediate cause could only be the attention which Henry Benton had shown me. His insinuation had been that I remained too much a little girl, and I had shown him that at any rate I was a bold, or at least a naughty, little girl.

My father was on his feet. He put his glasses on the mantelpiece. It seemed to me that from the three men came in rapid succession all possible arrangements of the words, boys-come-in. Come-in-boys.

Well-boys-come-in. Come-on-in. Boys-come-in-the-parlor. The boys went in, rather showing off their breeding and poise, I thought.

The three men moved and talked clumsily before them, as the three Benton brothers went each to each of the men carefully distinguishing between my uncles' titles: doctor and colonel.

I thought how awkward all the members of my own family appeared on occasions that called for grace.

Brother strode into the room with his hunting cap sideways on his head, and he announced their plans, which the tactful Benton's, uncertain of our family's prejudices regarding machines, had not mentioned.

Father and my uncles had a great deal to say about who was going-to-do-the-driving, and Henry Benton without giving an answer gave a polite invitation to the men to join them.

To my sorrow, both my uncles accepted with the greatest of pleasure what really had not been an invitation at all. They persisted in accepting it even after Brother in his rudeness raised the question of room in the five-passenger vehicle.

Father said, "Sure. The more, the merrier." But he declined to go himself and declined for me Henry's invitation.

The plan was, then, as finally outlined by the oldest of the Benton brothers, that the boys should proceed to the Carltons' and that brother should return with the driver to take our uncles out to the Carltons' house which was one of the new residences across from Centennial Park, where the excursions in the machine were to be made.

The four slender youths took their leave from the heavy men with the gold watch chains across their stomachs, and I had to shake hands with each of the Benton brothers.

To each, I expressed my regret that Father would not let me ride with them, mimicking their poise with all my art.

Henry Benton was the last, and he smiled as though he knew what I was up to. In answer to his smile I said, "Games are so much fun."

I stood by the window watching the four boys in the street until they were out of sight.

My father and his brothers had taken their seats in silence, and I was aware of just how unwelcome I was in the room.

Finally, my uncle who had been a colonel in the Spanish War and who wore bushy blond sideburns whistled under his breath and said, "Well, there's no doubt about it, no doubt about it."

He winked at my father, and my father looked at me and then at my uncle. Then quickly in a ridiculously over-serious tone he asked, "What, sir? No doubt about what, sir?"

"Why, there's no doubt that this daughter of yours was flirting with the youngest of the Messrs. Benton."

My father looked at me and twisted his mustache and said with the same pomp that he didn't know what he'd do with me if I started that sort of thing.

My two uncles threw back their heads, each giving a short laugh. My uncle the doctor took off his pince-nez and shook them at me and spoke in the same mock-serious tone of his brothers.

"Young lady, if you spend your time in such pursuits, you'll only bring upon yourself and upon the young men about Nashville the greatest unhappiness.

I, as a bachelor, must plead the cause of the young Benton's!"

I turned to my father in indignation and approached rage.

"Father," I shouted, "there's Mr. Smith out there!"

Father sprang from his chair and quickly stepped up beside me at the window.

Then, seeing the old man staggering harmlessly along the sidewalk, he said in, I thought, affected easiness.

"Yes. Yes, dear."

"He's drunk," I said. My lips quivered, and I think I must have blushed at this first mention of the unmentionable to my father.

"Poor Old Smith," he said. I looked at my uncles, and they were shaking their heads, echoing my father's tone.

"Whatever did happen to Smith's old maid sister?" my uncle the doctor said.

"She's still with him," Father said.

Mr. Smith appeared soberer today than I had ever seen him. He carried no overcoat to drag on the ground, and his stagger was barely noticeable.

The movement of his lips and an occasional gesture were the only evidence of intoxication.

I was angered by the irony that his good behavior on this of all days presented.

Had I been a little younger, I might have suspected conspiracy on the part of all men against me, but I was old enough to suspect no person's being even interested enough in me to plot against my understanding, unless it be some vague personification of life itself.

The course which I took, I thought afterward, was the proper one. I do not think that it was because I was then conscious that when one is determined to follow some course rigidly and is blockaded one must fire furiously, if blindly, into the blockade, but rather because I was frightened and, in my fear, forgot all logic of attack.

At any rate, I fired furiously at the three immutable creatures.

"I'm afraid of him," I broke out tearfully. I shouted at them, "He's always drunk! He's always going by our house drunk!"

My father put his arms about me, but I continued talking as I wept on his shirt front, and I felt my father move one hand from my back to motion my uncles to go. As they shut the parlor door after them, I felt that I had let them escape me.

I heard the motor fading out up Church Street, and Father led me to the day bed. We sat there together for a long while, and neither of us spoke until my tears had dried.

I was eager to tell him just exactly how fearful I was of Mr. Smith's coming into our house. He only allowed me to tell him that I was afraid; for when I had barely suggested that much, he said that I had no business watching Mr. Smith, that I must shut my eyes to some things.

"After all," he said, nonsensically I thought, "you're a young lady now." In just several curiously twisted sentences, he told me that I mustn't seek things to fear in this world.

He said that it was most unlikely, besides, that Smith would ever have business at our house.

He punched at his left side several times, gave a prolonged belch, settled a pillow behind his head, and soon was sprawled beside me on the day bed, snoring.

Mr. Smith did come to our house, and it was less than two months after this dreary twilight.

He came as I had feared he might come, in his most extreme state of drunkenness and at a time when I was alone in the house with the maid Lucy.

I had done everything that a little girl, now fourteen, could do in preparation for such an eventuality.

The sort of preparation that I had been able to make, the clearance of all restraints and inhibitions regarding Mr. Smith I think, given me a mature view of my own limited experiences; though, too, my very age must be held to account for a natural step toward maturity.

In the two months that followed, the day that I first faced Mr. Smith's existence with my father, I came to look at every phase of our household life with a more direct and more discerning eye.

As I wandered about that shadowy and somehow brutally elegant house, sometimes now with a knot of hair on the back of my head, events, and customs there that had repelled or frightened me I gave the closest scrutiny.

In the daytime I ventured into such forbidden spots as the servants' and the men's bathrooms.

The filth of the former became a matter of interest in the study of the servants' natures, instead of the object of ineffable disgust.

The other became a fascinating place of wet shaving brushes and leather straps and red rubber bags.

There was an anonymous little Negro boy that I had seen many mornings hurrying away from our back door with a pail.

I discovered that he was holding buttermilk from our icebox with the permission of our cook.

I sprang at him from behind a corner of the house one morning and scared him so that he spilled the buttermilk and never returned for more.

Another morning I heard the cook threatening to slash the houseboy with her butcher knife, and I made myself burst in upon them; and before Lucy and the houseboy I told her that if she didn't leave our house that day, I'd call my father and, hardly knowing what I was saying, I added, "And the police."

She was gone, and Lucy had got a new cook before dinner time. This way, from day to day, I began to take my place as mistress in our motherless household.

I could no longer be frightened by my brother with a mention of runaway horses.

Instead of terrorized, I felt only depressed by his long and curious arguments with my father.

I was depressed by the number of the subjects to and from which they fluctuated. The world still seemed unconscionably larger than anything I could comprehend.

I had learned not to concern myself with so general and so unreal a problem until I had cleared up more particular and real ones.

It was during these two months that I noticed the difference between the way my father spoke before my uncles of Mr. Smith when he passed and that in which he spoke of him before my brother.

To my brother, it was the condemning, "There goes Old Smith again." To my uncles it was, "There goes Old Smith," with the sympathetic addition, "the rascal."

Though my father and his brothers obviously found me more agreeable because a pleasant spirit had replaced my old timidity, they yet considered me a child.

My father little dreamed that I distinguished such traits in his character, or that I understood, if I even listened to, their anecdotes and their long funny stories, and it was an interest in the peculiar choice of subject and in the way that the men told their stories.

When Mr. Smith came, I was accustomed to thinking that there was something in my brother's and in my father's nature that was fully in sympathy with the very brutality of his drunkenness.

I knew that they would not consider my hatred for him and for that part of him which I saw in them.

For that alone I was glad that it was on a Thursday afternoon, when I was in the house alone with Lucy, that one of the heavy sorts of rains that toward the end of May drove Mr. Smith onto on our porch for shelter.

Otherwise, I wished for nothing more than the sound of my father's strong voice when I stood trembling before the parlor window and watched Mr. Smith stumbling across our lawn in the blasting rain.

I only knew how to keep at the window and make sure that he was coming into our house. I believe that he was drunker than I had ever before seen him, and his usual ire seemed to be doubled by the raging weather.

Despite the aid of his cane, Mr. Smith fell to his knees once in the muddy sod. He remained kneeling there for a time with his face cast in resignation.

Then once more, he struggled to his feet in the rain. Though I was ever conscious that I was entering into young womanhood at that age, I can only think of myself as a child at that moment; for it was the helpless fear of a child that I felt as I watched Mr. Smith approaching our door.

Perhaps it was the last time I ever experienced the inconsolable desperation of childhood.

Next, I could hear his cane beating on the boarding of the little porch before our door.

I knew that he must be walking up and down in that little shelter. Then I heard Lucy's exasperated voice as she came down the steps.

I knew immediately, what she confirmed afterward, that she thought it Brother, eager to get into the house, beating on the door.

I, shocked, opened the parlor door just as she pulled open the great front door. Her black skin ashened as she beheld Mr. Smith, his face crimson, his eyes bleary, and his gray clothes dripping water.

He shuffled through the doorway and threw his stick on the hall floor. Between his oaths and profanities, he shouted over and over in his broken, old man's voice, "Nigger, nigger."

I could understand little of his rapid and slurred speech, but I knew his rage went round and round a man in the rain and the shelter of a neighbor's house.

Lucy fled up the long flight of steps and was on her knees at the head of the stairs, in the dark upstairs hall, begging me to come up to her.

I only stared, as though paralyzed and dumb, at him and then up the steps at her. The front door was still open; the hall was half in light;

and I could hear the rain on the roof of the porch and the wind blowing on the trees which were in full green foliage.

At last, I moved. I acted. I slid along the wall past the hat rack and the console table, my eyes on the drunken old man who was swearing up the steps at Lucy.

I reached for the telephone; and when I had rung for central, I called the police station.

I knew what they did with Mr. Smith downtown, and I knew with what I had threatened the cook.

There was a part of me that was crouching on the top step with Lucy, vaguely longing to hide my face from this in my own mother's bosom.

There was another part which was making me deal with Mr. Smith, however wrongly, myself.

Innocently, I asked the voice to send "the Black Maria" to our house number on Church Street.

Mr. Smith had heard me make the call. He was still and silent for just one moment.

Then, he burst into tears, and he seemed to be chanting his words. He repeated the word "child" so many times that I felt I had acted wrongly, with courage but without wisdom.

I saw myself as a little beast adding to the injury that what was bestial in man had already done him.

He picked up his cane and didn't seem to be talking either to Lucy or to me, but to the cane.

He started out the doorway, and I heard Lucy come running down the stairs. She fairly glided around the newel post and passed me to the telephone.

She wasn't certain that I had made the call. She asked if I had called my father. I simply told her that I had not.

As she rang the telephone, I watched Mr. Speed cross the porch. He turned to us at the edge of the porch and shouted one more oath.

His foot touched the wet porch step, and he slid and fell unconscious on the steps.

He lay there with the rain beating upon him and with Lucy and myself watching him, motionless from our place on the telephone.

I was frightened by the thought of the cruelty which I found I was capable of, a cruelty which seemed inextricably mixed with what I had called courage.

I looked at him lying out there in the rain and despised and pitied him at the same time, and I was afraid to go minister to the helpless old Mr. Smith.

Lucy had her arms about me and kept them there until two gray horses pulling their black coach had galloped up in front of the house and two policemen had carried the limp body through the rain to the dreadful vehicle.

Just as the policemen closed the doors in the back of the coach, my father rode up in a closed cab.

He jumped out and stood in the rain for several minutes arguing with the policemen. Lucy and I went to the door and waited for him to come in.

When he came, he didn't look at either of us. He walked past us saying only, "I regret that the bluecoats were called." And he went into the parlor and closed the door.

I never discussed the events of that day with my father, and I never saw Mr. Smith again.

Despite the surge of pity, I felt for the old man on our porch that afternoon, my hatred, and fear of what he had stood for in my eyes has never left me.

Since that day that I watched myself say "away" in the mirror, not a week has passed but that he has been brought to my mind by one thing or another.

It was only the other night that I dreamed I was a little girl on Church Street again and that there was a drunk horse in our yard...

CHAPTER 3

The Representations of Spinsters

This focuses on a group of female characters who have never been married and whose role within Irish society is, therefore, not defined by marriage or child rearing.

This about Irish female writers whose works cover, overall, the entire second half of the twentieth century.

They are Mary Lavin in the pre-1960's, Maeve Kelly, Emma Cooke, Clare Boylan, Jan Kennedy in the 1970's and 80's, Mary Beckett, Angela Bourke, and Claire Keegan in the 1990's.

Running through the works of these writers is a core theme of generalized hostility within Irish society towards women who, by choice or circumstance, have remained single.

The stories by these writers return consistently to portrayals of the force exerted upon women by society to conform through self-sacrifice in a cultural environment which emphasizes the benefit of society in general at the expense of women.

These stories examine the social ideology underlying and underpinning the politics of gender roles and human interaction within Irish society.

The stories achieve this goal by choosing themes and issues of alienation, internal exile, and prejudice against spinsters, and setting these against a backdrop of an ideological manifestation of a "spinsters as odd women" stereotype as well as of a requirement for women to conform to a role of selfless "social mothers".

The social norm shaping women into natural wives and mothers serves, in effect, as a means of social control over women, Mustard 2004 "Spinster".

Representations of a negative image of single women as spinsters in these stories indicate the continuing social marginalization and discrimination which this distinctive, single woman, group experiences because of falling outside of the conventional social enclosure in Ireland.

The social phenomenon in post-famine Ireland in which a growing number of women stayed unmarried or permanently celibate is not unique in the context of modern Western Europe.

Like other western European countries, Ireland also experienced rural depopulation. Given that Ireland was, and remains, a stronghold of the belief that the role of women lay in domesticity and motherhood, a belief reinforced by the rejection of birth control of any kind, it is worth noting that the demographic patterns of population growth in Ireland since the Great Famine up to the 1960s remained much lower than in many other European countries.

Partly, this demographic pattern may be due to "the combined effects of large-scale emigration and the lowest marriage rate in Europe", Murphy-Lawless 1993.

The feasibility of attaining married status for Irish men and women may also have been limited in many respects by practical factors and available economic options.

The tightening economic conditions resulted in a gradual change in the system of land inheritance amongst rural farmers.

Typically, only the eldest son could inherit his father's land and therefore only the eldest son would have been in a practical position to marry and raise a family of his own.

As a result, the younger siblings either had to stay single or leave, or possibly both, Clarkson 1981, Strassman and Clark 1998.

At that time, many single women left the country to escape poverty and perhaps also social pressure resulting from their continuing single status, Horgan 2001 "Women's Lives".

The 1937 Constitution emphasizes that the primary role of women in Irish society was that of wife and mother, a reflection of a dominant view that "the family was a moral institution, possessing inalienable and imprescriptible rights", Murphy-Lawless 1993.

Marriage in general becomes the social norm, or default option, for women because women are largely defined in Irish society by the roles and duties in which they engage within the enclosure of marriage.

Even today, social identities of Irish women continue to be constructed in the domestic arena of marriage and motherhood despite Ireland's economic modernization as a member of the European Community, a theoretical availability of greater choice to women through access to higher education, and the impact of women's movements, Byrne 2008.

Pat O'Connor argues that the domestic roles of Irish women such as caring, reproduction and family management are deemed by the state and the church to be "key elements in the definition of womanhood.

Love and sexual attraction… effectively obscure the issue of state control", O'Connor 1998.

This is also the picture which comes through in many representations of the, seemingly more or less obligatory, pursuit of love alongside marriage in contemporary Irish women's short stories.

However, there is a double-bind paradox underpinning this seemingly central status of marriage and family in Irish society.

On the one hand, the state and the church emphasize the essential role of family and motherhood.

On the other hand, the ideologically based sexual repression supported by Irish politics and Catholicism was a contributory factor in the patterns of late marriage and permanent celibacy which seemed to "become the norm in Ireland" until the second half of the 20th century, Horgan 2001 "Women's Lives".

This odd phenomenon in Ireland is also mirrored in Irish women's stories in which some women do not stay celibate or single by choice but do so under duress from circumstances beyond their control.

Chapter 4

Spinsters as Odd Neurotic

Anne Byrne, an Irish sociologist at NUI Galway, starts her chapter "Single women in Ireland" in Women on Their Own: Interdisciplinary Perspectives on Being Single, 2008, as follows:

Single women, born in the 1950s and 1960s, reveal the identity effects of the ideology of marriage and family that continues to resonate in contemporary Irish society despite the economic and social forces of modernity.

Feministic ideologies positively support constructions of womanhood as married and mother, a context in which singlehood and the opposition between woman identity and single identity are problematic.

In the absence of positive and powerful counternarratives, singlehood is disparaged and stigmatized, constraining the identity possibilities for all women, Byrne 2008.

Byrne's study identifies a clear association of women's singlehood, even in contemporary Ireland, with social inadequacy and exclusion.

Single women can be seen to form a group clearly "marked by 'social sufferings', a consequence of their nonconformity to the cultural hegemony of marriage and family.

The spinster stereotype as manifested in Irish women's stories may be easier to analyze if we first consider the term spinster and its associations within the cultural contexts of western societies.

The term "spinsters" originally referred to women who worked as spinners to earn their own living, and then evolved into a synonym for those who are usually long past their "sell-by date" for marriage and thus had to earn their keep in the parental home by spinning and weaving.

Although semantically the primary definition of the term spinster is someone, usually a woman, who spins thread or yarn, or who practices spinning as a regular occupation, according to both the New Oxford Dictionary of English and the Webster's New World Dictionary of the American Language, the secondary definition refers to a woman who is beyond the usual age for marriage, in other words, an old maid.

The word spinster may even be used in a secondary, negative way to refer to single women in general, Weigle 1982.

This term, spinster, which first appeared as a designation of an unmarried woman (regardless of whether young or old) in court documents in England in medieval times, has been associated with negative images of women in the literature of Protestant England since the 18th century and this negative association seems subsequently to have spread to other European countries and to America, Froide 2005.

The resulting growth in social anxiety due to the rising number of single women transformed the spinster in media and literature into a negative caricature implying women who are typically middle-aged, eccentric, ill-natured, selfish, or even evil.

Nevertheless, in the late 19th century, when the first wave of feminism began to spread widely across Europe and America, this traditionally negative term was once adopted by feminist activists such as Cicely Hamilton in a way that had a positive association, as part of a political strategy targeted against the tyrannical, male-dominated marriage institution and mandatory heterosexuality, Hamilton 1909.

Jeffreys 1985, This Victorian feminist rejection of an unjust marriage system finds echoes amongst contemporary Irish female writers in many of their depictions of women's lives which deal with what Irene Boada-Montegut has termed compulsory marriage.

The status quo of gender politics is secured once women are forced into marriage and family, and therefore must obey.

If women fall, for whatever reason, outside this domain, they risk either being demonized or expelled as social outcasts to intimidate younger women into not following a similar path.

Single women also tend to be forced to adopt a surrogate mothering role as carers, which once again limits women's scope to pursue the same life or career options as their male counterparts.

Hence, female characters in Irish women's stories are sometimes forced by circumstances to become spinsters because they are pressurized to give up their lives, including marriage, and serve their parents at home.

This seems ironic when compared to the stereotype which assumes that spinsters simply stay home as parasites because they are selfish enough to run away from their predestined childbearing responsibility to family and society.

A spinster may be represented stereotypically as a comic, grotesque, ugly, dull woman, or as an alienated misfit who displays a pitiful prudery and who is incapable of a human connection due to her "failure" to achieve a relationship with a man, Auerbach 1982.

M. Haskell describes the collective image of the spinster stereotype as follows:

Like witch, spinster, was a scare word, a stereotype that served to embrace and isolate a group of women of vastly different dispositions, talents, situations, but whose common bond, never having become half of a pair, was enough to throw into question the rules and presumed priorities on which society was founded, Haskell 1988.

The main underlying factor in the social isolation which characterizes the literary portrayals of single women appears to be that people either dislike or fear them.

As a result, they are excluded. They are even portrayed as evil witchlike figures.

The spinster stereotype also tends to mock and demonize the single woman as one who is barren, "frumpy, middle-aged" or "somewhat depressed, and is longing to be like other normal women" [italics my own], Mustard 2004 "Spinster".

The image of a pathetic, neurotic, single woman who envies and longs to be like other normal women is another aspect of the stereotype. From this point of view, a single woman's life is never complete without marriage.

The idea that a single woman can enjoy a fulfilled life outside marriage is inevitably looked upon with suspicion by the general majority within society.

CHAPTER 5

Clara the Spinster

It was during the summer of her 20th birthday when Lydia met her two best friends, Virginia, and Luz. The three girls were destined to share the same fate of becoming spinsters.

They would eventually meet their Casanovas in their very own strange ways....

On this day, they were out on the playground of their elementary school, swinging on the monkey bars. Lilly, who had never really had any real friends before, asked herself this very odd question that had been boggling her mind for a while.

"Friends. What are they for?"

Luz, with her sunny blond hair and bright sky-blue eyes, seemed very eager to meet people.

Virginia was always explaining stuff to her friends. She explains that a father was there to protect you. The mother is dear to wipe your tears and make you happy.

"Is that all?" Lilly asked in wonder, her dark-brown eyes large.

"There's more! There's more!" Virginia said, hopping in her spot, eager for her friends to listen to her very wise words, her braided hair bouncing about.

Then she proceeded to dance and clap her hands like a monkey. "Friends are always there with you, always around you, like right now. I'm happy.

I'm clapping my hands because I have my friends with me. Clap with me, Lilly." She grinned. "Clap with me, Luz." She urged them to clap and dance with her.

The clueless two happily followed her lead and began clapping their hands and dancing silly dances, like clowns in a circus.

"See, friends make each other look like fools, but they still have fun," Virginia said wisely.

"So, will you promise to be my teddy bear, my comfort pillow, my favorite blankie, and Kleenex tissue, then?" Clara asked her two friends.

"Sure," Viginia said.

"You bet on it," Luz replied.

"Promise?" Lillie wanted to make sure they weren't going to run out on her.

After all, she knew no one else wanted to be her friend, since she was so different.

"Promise" Luz and Virginia said in harmony.

"Let's pinky swear, then," Lillie suggested.

"Yes, pinky swear," Vivian said, grinning.

Luz nodded in agreement.

Clarice entwined her left pinky with Whitney's. On the right side, she entwined with Elisa's left, while Elisa had her right pinky with Whitney's left. In turn, the three friends formed a circle, an endless unity of friendship.

"We promise to be great friends. We promise to pick each other up when the other falls. We promise to be your teddy bear, your favorite blankie and your Kleenex tissue.

We promise to laugh with you when you laugh. We are sisters as well as friends. From now on, we are one."

Then they leaned forward until all three foreheads touched.

"Friends," they all said in harmony. Then they pulled back and smiled their cheesy, toothy smiles at each other.

When the door opened, a naked torso faced Clara. Not just any old torso, but a hot, muscled, six-pack naked torso.

She blinked and blinked, and then she blinked some more.

She couldn't understand why a grown man would be wearing a towel, just a single white, fluffy towel wrapped around his waist, to answer the door.

He was leaning against the doorframe, one hand supporting his tall, lean, muscular body that, Clara noted, any female would want in her bed, including her.

Not that she'd bedded any male, of course, since she was still a bloody virgin, for God's sake.

As her eyes traveled up to his face, her heart decided to do a disco dance, moving in time to the sound of the very popular music currently playing in the background somewhere inside the man's house.

She felt a little breathless and lightheaded. Her cheeks flushed the same shade as the bouquet of scarlet roses in her arms.

Not that she was florist or a delivery person or anything. No, the florist was one of her best friends, Elisa, and the delivery person was too sick with influenza.

So being the great best friend that she was, Clara offered to help.

Elisa had begged because this was her VIP client. Elisa herself was too busy preparing for the many orders for Valentine's Day, which was tomorrow, so the job was thrust upon her with little room for argument.

Clara herself had succumbed to Elisa's bribery of free roses, which she really loved.

Now here she was, knocking on the door of 99 Smith Street in Brooklyn, NY. Her eyes were busy blinking rapidly at the half-naked male specimen standing before her.

My oh my, did she almost forget she was holding on to the bunch of roses because, heaven help her, this man was G-O-R-G-E-O-U-S.

That slightly wet, dusted-corn hair had a sparkling golden sheen beneath the afternoon sunlight.

The man looked so hot she couldn't help looking at him.

Putting all the symptoms together, which included the pronounced asthma induced breaths, the after-the-marathon heart rate, and the light-as-a-feather feeling inside her head and stomach.

Clara concluded this condition was since she had never seen a naked man in the flesh in her whole twenty-nine years of life.

If she had counted the time, she had seen her young nephews during their bath time, however, then yes, maybe she had seen the male species displaying their valued male anatomies.

For the likes of men like this one, so well-toned, so well made, and with so much testosterone, then the answer would be a definite no.

Those arms looked so strong, so muscular, so....

"Can I help you?" he asked, drawing her senses back to reality, breaking the spell, and making her blink a few more times before she became aware of the mission she came to accomplish.

"Umm." Suddenly, she realized she'd lost her voice. Her throat was dry as dust.

She tried to speak, but the only sound that came out was, "Umm..." again. Knowing any attempt to speak again would only make her sound more of a complete idiot, she resorted to using hand gestures.

Clara practically shoved the bouquet right in his gorgeous face. That took him by surprise, and he moved backward.

"So... sorry," she croaked. There, finally, she'd found her voice. Even though it didn't sound anything like her natural voice, at least she could pass her message across verbally.

"No, that's fine. Just a little startled, that's all."

Gosh, this man has such a nice voice, she couldn't help thinking.

"Darling, what's taking so long?" A singsong voice traveled from somewhere inside the house. "Come back to bed."

The hottie turned to smile at whoever it was, then said softly, "Be back soon."

He has such soft eyes, Clara thought when he turned to smile at the woman, she assumed to be his wife.

They were azure blue, like a clear, cloudless summer sky.

Dear heaven! Why are all good and handsome men taken? They were like car parks.

All the good and available ones were taken, whereas the ones that were available were the ones you had to parallel park to get. Damn my parallel parking.

His attention suddenly shifted back to Clara, and what she saw written on his face she did not like.

His once soft and experienced azure eyes that had spoken of gentleman breed had now completely vanished.

In its place shone a glittering spark, those pupils displaying a strong, wicked gleam, like the devil about to play with his toy.

His once broad and friendly smile had also been completely wiped away.

Instead, the corners of those lips quirked up to form a devilish grin.

Danger! Danger! Playboy alert! Clara's radar screamed at her when those wicked eyes started undressing her, causing her scarlet cheeks to burn even more.

Before she could take a step back to assess her situation, the man caught hold of the bouquet, capturing her hands in the process.

"Hey, let… let go." She struggled, trying to remove his tight grasp.

"Naaaoooohhh." He shook his head, that devilish grin still plastered on his face, his eyes still sparkling with mischief.

Clara tried harder to release his vise like grip, but it was no use. His fingers were like dental clamps, wrapped around her hands so securely one would require pliers to release them.

"I said…" Clara couldn't finish her sentence, as she almost stumbled backward when the man suddenly released her.

"Why?" She was about to give him a piece of her mind when he interrupted her yet again, and she was struck speechless.

"You like what you see?" he asked, posing even more seductively on the threshold of the doorframe, contorting his body as if he were a model out of Vogue magazine.

"Huh? Excuse me?" Clara asked, puzzled.

"Obviously you came here to give me these roses," his voice drawled out huskily.

"You must like me; otherwise, you wouldn't be here. Valentine's Day isn't until tomorrow."

"I…" Once again, her speech was interrupted when she saw a blonde entering her field of vision, striking a pose as fashionable as the man before her.

The woman leaned onto the man and gave him a peck on the cheek, unaware to Clara's presence.

The woman proceeded to move down to the man's lips, making a sucking sound like a fish out of water, then to his Adam's apple, until the man cleared his throat, drawing her attention to the fact that they had a guest.

Clara's eyeballs almost dropped to the floor when the blonde turned to face her.

She too was only dressed in a loose towel, covering just enough for her breasts not to spill out.

The woman eyed her briefly. Then sensing Clara had the same significance as the potted plant displayed on the front porch; she turned back to her man.

"Carlos, honey," she whined and then kissed Hunter right in front of her again.

"You took way too long, so I had to come and get you."

Carlos didn't look like he was interested. His eyes were roaming elsewhere, and Clara just happened to be their target.

Gosh, get a room, you two! Clara wanted to yell at them for being this intimate in broad daylight.

Why am I still here anyway? Her job was done. She should get going. Somehow, though, she wanted to get even with this blasted Carlos, who was still grinning at her flirtatiously.

As if on cue, the blonde turned to her, giving her an evil glare. She said, "Why are you still here? Who are you and what are you doing here, kid?"

KID? All right, that did it. Clara snapped. Who was this chick calling her a kid like she'd just been born yesterday?

She was almost thirty, for God's sake. This bimbo was clearly her junior by almost a decade and had no right whatsoever to insult her.

After all, she was very sensitive about her age, and her pride just couldn't take it when someone called attention to it.

Clara wanted to growl. This younger generation just didn't show respect to their elders.

She really needed to set the record straight. With that thought in mind, she tightened her fists tight in self-determination, lifted her head to meet their eyes, and said, "I'm here to...."

"To give me roses for Valentine's Day." Carlos grinned.

That did it.

"You bitch!" the blonde screeched, like an angry cat running its claws across a chalkboard, grating her eardrums.

If Clara were to stay around listening to this bimbo for another second, she could guarantee she'd lose her auditory senses.

What to do? she thought. That was when she saw Carlos's eyes again. There was that wicked gleam. That was when it came to her. She knew why he'd said all that stuff before about roses and Valentine's Day.

This blasted man wasn't this bimbo's husband. They were merely playmates. Oh, what was she saying? Why use neutral term?

They'd practically just had sex moments before she knocked on the door, and now, if she suspected right, Carlos wanted to break up with the blonde and he was using Clara as his outlet.

Not so fast, you handsome beast. You're not getting away this easy. Before the blonde could do further damage to her eardrums and before her hot temper exploded like a boiling kettle, she threw the bouquet in Carlos's face.

She grabbed both their towels, one in each hand, and yanked them off their bodies, exposing his and her anatomies to the black cat sitting on the fence, birds in the trees, the bees sucking nectar from flowers on the porch, and whoever happened to glimpse them at that moment.

The blonde screamed, the man growled, and Clara twisted on her heel and ran for her life, running like the devil had taken chase.

Of course, she knew the devil would never come chasing after her in his naked state. But she did stop to catch her breath when she was halfway down the block because her limbs refused to take another step for fear of her lungs collapsing.

Wow! Clara couldn't believe she'd just done that, yanking off their towels like that.

Then, she began to laugh so hard her stomach hurt. Once she managed to calm down, she thought it was a shame she'd been too busy making her escape to clearly see his male glory.

Stop thinking stupid thoughts this instant!

What was with her and her sudden fascination with the male anatomy anyway?

Was it because her biological clock was ticking, telling her it was almost time for her to start thinking about producing some babies? Good Lord, she wasn't looking forward to her big three-zero.

How was she supposed to make babies if her forbidden door downstairs had yet to be unlocked? And worse yet, where was she supposed to find the right key for her door?

A naughty thought ran through her head. Maybe Carlos had a secret key to unlock my door?

Then her heart did a little tumble. Ah! She messed up her hair in her thought process. Calm down, my dear heart.

She placed her hand upon her chest to stop the thrashing beat of her heart. Otherwise, she might have gone into cardiac arrest, and there was no hospital near this part of town.

Once her heart settled again, her thoughts returned to the blond-haired, azure blue-eyed Carlos.

What was she thinking that he might have the right key for her door?

That beast was a playboy, a Casanova, who saw women as nothing above a piece of bacon.

That shaggy dog man-beast, eyeing her like a steak, wanting a piece of her.

Well, he wasn't getting a piece, even if this steak was getting old, like tough leather old.

Clara sighed in defeat. There was no point in sulking over matters like this now.

She must call Elisa tonight to apologize for the turn of events. Elisa might lose one VIP client, but it was better for her staff not to be harassed or taken advantage of by that Casanova Carlos.

Dropping the thought for later use, Clara turned to walk back to her car. Her shoulders slumping, mentally counting down the days until she meets her doomsday.

But that day came faster than she expected....

REFERENCES

"Spinster", Merriam-Webster Dictionary

"Spinster". WordReference.com. Retrieved 2 April 2016.

Douglas Harper (2010). "Spinster defined". Online Etymology Dictionary. Dictionary.com Unabridged. Retrieved 5 June 2014.

"John West, Sexual Offences: assault with intent". Old Bailey Proceedings Online. 13 December 1699. Retrieved 28 July 2012. for assaulting on Mary Bowden, Spinster, a Virgin, under the Age of Ten Years

"Marriage service rubric". The Book of Common Prayer.

"Spinster defined". American English. Oxford Dictionaries. Archived from the original on 14 December 2012. Retrieved 11 June 2014.

"Webster's Revised Unabridged Dictionary (1913 + 1828)". Archived from the original on 22 February 2014. Retrieved 8 November 2012.

Berend, Zsuzsa (2000). "'The Best or None!' Spinsterhood in Nineteenth-Century New England". Journal of Social History. 33 (4): 935–957. doi:10.1353/jsh.2000.0056. PMID 18050547. S2CID 40799246.

"Spinster definition". Merriam-Webster. Retrieved 5 June 2014.

"Spinster defined". Based on the Random House Dictionary, © Random House, Inc. Dictionary.com Unabridged. 2014. Retrieved 5 June 2014.

"Spinster". WordReference.com. Retrieved 19 October 2016.

Lakoff, Robin (1975). Language and Woman's Place. New York: Harper and Row. ISBN 9780060903893.

Jeffreys, Sheila (1985). The Spinster and Her Enemies: Feminism and Sexuality 1880–1930. ISBN 9780863580505.

Bielski, Zosia (7 May 2015). "In her new book, Kate Bolick argues why there's nothing wrong with being a 'spinster'". The Globe and Mail.

"R.I.P bachelor's and Spinsters". BBC. 14 September 2005. Retrieved 8 April 2013.

"Single Women Still Feel Spinster Stigma, Study Finds". LiveScience. March 2010.

Sharp, Elizabeth A.; Ganong, Lawrence (2011). "'I'm a Loser, I'm Not Married, Let's Just All Look at Me': Ever-Single Women's Perceptions of Their Social Environment". Journal of Family Issues. 32 (7): 956–980. doi:10.1177/0192513X10392537. S2CID 146368386.

"Louisa May Alcott, Spinster, Enjoys Valentine's Day 1868". New England Historical Society. 14 February 2015. Retrieved 19 October 2016.

Hill, Bridget (2001). Women Alone Spinsters in England 1660-1850. Yale University Press. p. 10. ISBN 0300088205.

Nicholson, Virginia (2007). Singled Out: How Two Million Women Survived Without Men After the First World War.

Harder, Arlene (2009). The Developmental Stages of Erik Erikson.

Schwartz, Pepper (15 October 2014). "Why more women choose not to marry". CNN.

Rich, Adrienne (1980). "Compulsory Heterosexuality and Lesbian Existence". Signs: Journal of Women in Culture and Society. 5 (4): 631–660. doi:10.1086/493756. S2CID 143604951.

Flah, Loubna (18 August 2012). "'Bayrat' or 'Spinsters', Single Women Trapped in Social Stigma". Morocco World News.

Orenstein, Peggy (1 July 2001), "Parasites in Prêt-à-Porter", The New York Times

Wiseman, Paul (2 June 2004), "No sex please – we're Japanese", USA Today, retrieved 3 January 2013, Better educated, more widely travelled, and raised in more affluence than their mothers, young women no longer feel bound by the Japanese tradition that says a woman unmarried after age 25 is like a Christmas cake on Dec. 26 — stale.

"Spinsters of San Francisco". sfspinsters.com. Retrieved 14 April 2015.

"The Merry Spinster: Reclaiming the Pejorative: Too Much Talky". 3 March 2014. Archived from the original on 3 March 2014.

Zeisler, Andi (27 November 2012). "The Big Feminist BUT: Corinne Mucha's 'Spinster'". Bitch Magazine.

"Spinster House" – via YouTube.

Cat Ladies

@everywhereist (7 December 2019). "The most unrealistic part about "It's a Wonderful Life" isn't the angel stuff but the part where we must pretend…" (Tweet) – via Twitter.

Motteux, Peter Antony; Rabelais, François (1694). Gargantua and Pantagruel, The Fifth Book. Retrieved 22 March 2019.

Peter Motteux. Oxford English Dictionary. Archived from the original on 22 March 2019. Retrieved 22 March 2019.

Earl, Alice Morse (1894). Customs and Fashions in Old New England. Retrieved 22 March 2019.

Dunton, John (1705). The Life and Errors of John Dunton, Citizen of London: With the Lives and Characters of More... Retrieved 22 March 2019.

Viney, Michael (4 March 2017). "The fish disappearing from Irish waters". The Irish Times. Archived from the original on 25 December 2018. Retrieved 23 March 2019.

Memoirs of the Wernerian Natural History Society Volume 1. 1811. Retrieved 23 March 2019.

Thornback (1888 ed.). Oxford English Dictionary. 3 July 2014.

"Family of origin defined". Mosby's Medical Dictionary. 2009. Retrieved 2 June 2014.

Phelps, Pauline (1897). "Spinster Thurber's Carpet". Peterson's Magazine.

"Miss Marple Series". PBS, www.pbs.org.

Bush, William J. (2013). Greenback Dollar: The Incredible Rise of the Kingston Trio. Rowman & Littlefield. p. 224. ISBN 9780810881921.

Bolick, K. (2016). Spinster: Making a Life of One's Own. Crown. p. 260. ISBN 978-0-385-34715-0. Retrieved 14 April 2023.

Bryant, C.D. (2014). Deviant Behaviors: Readings in The Sociology Of Norm Violations. Taylor & Francis. p. 580. ISBN 978-1-317-77054-1. Retrieved 14 April 2023.

ABOUT THE AUTHOR

Norma Iris Pagan Morales was born in Ponce, Puerto Rico. She comes from a very lovable family. Her parents, Juan Jose Pagan Rodriguez, and Digna Morales Figueroa, now deceased, always helped her with her projects as a writer and teaching career.

Norma had three siblings, Adelin Milagros Pagan Morales, Juan Jose Pagan Morales, and Julio Manuel Pagan Morales. Julio Manuel Pagan Morales died on September 19, 1998, and My dear sister Adelin Milagros Pagan Morales died on February 17, 2023.

Norma did all her academic studies in New York City, Puerto Rico, and Canada. She worked in the City of New York Police Department. As an Educator, she worked in New York City Bd. of Education as an English Teacher, in Puerto Rico Bd. of Education as an English teacher and in the Puerto Rico Army National.

She has teaching certifications for English as a Second Language and Teaching English as a Foreign Language.

She had published thirteen books: Proud of My Puerto Rican Bequest, ¿Porque Soy Boricua? Poemas del Alma, Art in Written Form, A Baffling Short Stories Collection, On Job in the Big Apple, Puerto Rican Soldiers Serving with Pride, Nature's Rage in the Caribbean, Boricua de Pura Cepa, You are the One, The Unfaithfuls, Christopher Columbus and Violence in the City.